"Why do you want to work here?"

"I can't let my *aenti* pay all my expenses while I'm here. I'd just need work for a few weeks," Eva explained.

"Still, you don't seem so sure," Tanner replied.

"I'm sure about the work, but not so sure about working for you."

The woman who'd called him out to meet Eva snorted.

"I just don't know about this, Eva. I don't know you."

"Then never mind," she said, turning to leave. "I'll find work elsewhere."

After she heard what could have been a shove, Tanner appeared behind her. "Wait."

Eva turned to see Martha behind him, mouthing *please*. With a grin.

Eva smiled, causing Tanner to look back at his cousin. "Martha—I mean, Martha *and I*—would like to have you work here with us. If you want to do that, Martha will train you to work out front with the customers. Would that be suitable?"

Customers. She'd be around all sorts of people. What if she got sick again? What if *Mamm* found out?

What if she didn't try?

With over seventy books published and millions in print, **Lenora Worth** writes award-winning romance and romantic suspense. Three of her books finaled in the ACFW Carol Awards, and her Love Inspired Suspense novel *Body of Evidence* became a *New York Times* bestseller. Her novella in *Mistletoe Kisses* made her a *USA TODAY* bestselling author. Lenora goes on adventures with her retired husband, Don, and enjoys reading, baking and shopping…especially shoe shopping.

Books by Lenora Worth

Love Inspired

Pinecraft Seasons

Pinecraft Refuge

Amish Seasons

Their Amish Reunion
Seeking Refuge
Secrets in an Amish Garden

Men of Millbrook Lake

Lakeside Hero
Lakeside Sweetheart
Her Lakeside Family

Texas Hearts

A Certain Hope
A Perfect Love
A Leap of Faith

Visit the Author Profile page at LoveInspired.com for more titles.

Pinecraft Refuge

Lenora Worth

LOVE INSPIRED

INSPIRATIONAL ROMANCE

LOVE INSPIRED®

INSPIRATIONAL ROMANCE

ISBN-13: 978-1-335-58560-8

Pinecraft Refuge

Copyright © 2023 by Lenora H. Nazworth

For questions and comments about the quality of this book, please contact us at CustomerService@Harlequin.com.

Love Inspired
22 Adelaide St. West, 41st Floor
Toronto, Ontario M5H 4E3, Canada
www.LoveInspired.com

Printed in U.S.A.

Thus saith the Lord, which giveth the sun for a light by day, and the ordinances of the moon and of the stars for a light by night, which divideth the sea when the waves thereof roar; The Lord of hosts is his name.

—*Jeremiah* 31:35

To Florida, the Sunshine State
and a beautiful place to live!

Chapter One

Eva Miller stepped off the Elite Coach bus and inhaled the fresh, clean air of the Gulf of Mexico. Amazed that such a warm, sunny place as Pinecraft, Florida, existed after she'd left the February snow of Campton Creek, Pennsylvania, Eva smiled. And coughed.

Had there ever been a time when she didn't cough or sneeze or feel like she couldn't breathe? Constant allergies and respiratory problems had plagued her all of her life.

She missed Mamm, but the doctor had suggested some time away from the brutal winter temperatures and the heavy winter snow. "Let's send you to Florida for a while, Eva. You need to get completely well. This last bout of bronchitis caused pneumonia and we sure don't want that to happen again. You and your *mamm* are always talking about your aunt down there. I say go and visit her, rest and enjoy the fresh ocean air."

So here she stood after a trip that had lasted close to fifteen hours. She'd left last night, slept on the bus and was now wide awake at one in the afternoon. And hungry. Her breakfast had been the last of the snacks Mamm had packed in a small lunch box.

But she had to wait for someone to pick her up.

Her *aenti* Ramona Bauer had been so excited when she'd received Mamm's letter, she'd called the phone booth located on the main road in Campton Creek and left a message for them. "*Ja, kumm*, both of you. I'd love that."

Her *aenti* lived in Pinecraft year-round and had been inviting them for years. But Mamm didn't want to visit Florida or any other state for that matter. She loved her tiny home and had never remarried after Daed died when Eva was a toddler. Helen Miller was a homebody who loved to knit, read her Bible and a few novels and sew clothes for other people.

"I have sewing orders to complete, Eva. You'll have to go alone. Can you do that?"

She could do that, she'd assured her mother.

Eva had read many books about adventure and romance, and she longed to see the world. This would be a start if she didn't get sick again. And if Mamm would agree. Which she finally had.

"Only for a couple of months, Eva," Mamm had said after the doctor suggested the trip and Eva had wanted to get here and soon. "I do not like this idea, but I want you well. It's time to try something we haven't done before. I've always heard that sunshine and fresh air can help allergies and as the doctor would say, respiratory problems."

Eva had packed her medicine, some sanitized hand cream and wipes and the vitamins the doctor told her to continue taking. "Vitamin D and sunshine will help and eat a lot of fresh oranges while you're there," the doctor had suggested.

Sunshine. Oranges. Fresh air. The ocean. And in her mind, maybe more than a couple of months.

She smiled and took another breath, her eyes closed, the sense of peace inside her heart mixed with the anticipation of a true adventure.

Then she heard a man calling her name.

"Eva? Eva Miller?"

Eva glanced around to see several Amish on bicycles that looked like big tricycles with baskets attached. Where were the buggies? And who had called her name?

Tanner Dawson glanced around the busy bus station. The Tuesday run had arrived, and a group of Amish from Pennsylvania had filed off the bus. But which one was Eva Miller?

"You can't miss her," Romana Bauer had told him when she'd asked if he'd pick up her niece Eva. "She has the prettiest light brown hair and such sweet blue-green eyes, like my sister's. She's a bit frail and she'll be shy, so be kind to her, Tanner."

"I'm always kind," he'd told his friend in a gruff tone while he tried to smile.

Romana loved to match people and she'd been trying to match him up with a new wife for years. But he had no desire to remarry. He'd lost the woman he'd loved, but he had a beautiful daughter to keep him busy and happy.

Right now, he only wanted to get Eva to her *aenti*'s house so he could get back to his shop. Dawson Department Store wouldn't run itself. He'd left his cousin Martha in charge, and she was a bit scattered at times, but *gut* at selling his handmade driftwood products and beach supplies to all the tourists. Not so *gut* at being careful with the pieces he made by hand and sold. He'd forbidden her to go into his workshop. He'd hired a part-time Amish youth to help him carry and deliver the delicate driftwood pieces to customers all across Sarasota and the nearby islands. James was hardy and eager to learn wood crafting, and Tanner was eager to teach him.

Doing another scan, he noticed one lone young woman holding an old blue suitcase, her eyes wide and an unusual blue-green. Tanner moved through the crowd of people hugging and laughing as they reconnected. The Amish who lived here year-round often had relatives coming to visit during the winter when they didn't have crops to tend to, or if they wanted to get away from the cold and snow for a while.

This girl looked too fragile to lift hay bales or pick and preserve vegetables and fruit. She probably couldn't saddle a horse either. But they didn't have horses around here anyway.

"Eva?" he asked in a tentative pitch as he approached her.

"Ja," she said, her voice raspy and uncertain. "Who are you?"

The directness startled him, but Tanner didn't let her see that. He frowned—something Ramona and Martha told him he did a lot. "I'm Tanner Dawson. Your aunt sent me to get you." Grabbing her suitcase, he added, "Let's go."

He heard her winter boots hitting the pavement behind him. "Slow down," she called, sounding breathless. "Are we going to a fire?"

He nipped the smile that tried to escape and turned to face her. *"Neh,* but I have work to do."

"I'm sorry," she replied, a tad of spunk showing in her eyes. "I could have walked to my *aenti's* house."

"Neh," he replied. "Ramona asked me to come and fetch you. She said you were special and would need a ride."

"I'm nothing special," she replied, her words meek. "But where is your buggy?"

"Here," he said, pointing to the golf cart. Not that he played golf, but this was the best kind of taxi around this small Amish community sitting in the middle of Sarasota. "This is my buggy."

Eva balked and stared at the cart and then at him. "Is it safe?"

"As safe as any horse and buggy," he replied, his patience slipping away with each ticking second. "Or do you really want to walk with this suitcase?"

"Where should I sit?" she retorted, giving him his answer.

"Right here on the front seat, by me," he replied after placing her suitcase in the backseat. And instantly wished he hadn't said that with such force. "I don't bite," he added.

She climbed up onto the black vinyl bench seat and gave him a solemn stare. "Are you sure, because you're as burly as an old bear."

His lips twitched but he let the smile slide away. "I'm a very busy man, is all."

"Then get this thing moving. I'm starving and I don't like rude people."

"I wasn't rude." Was he?

"You weren't pleasant either, were you?"

Not used to such blunt talk, Tanner glanced over at her, aware of how close they were, being squeezed into this tiny cart. "Let me start over then. Hi, I'm Tanner. It's *gut* to meet you, Eva Miller. How long do you plan to stay in our paradise?"

She turned to slant her gaze toward him. "Well, if everyone here is as grumpy as you are, probably not long."

Eva had never met such a rude man. But then, she rarely met up with any boys or men, other than the ones she and Mamm would see at church. She'd attended youth functions and singings, but she wasn't the type to flirt. Her *rumspringa* had been disappointing since she hadn't gone out much and she sure had not acted up the way some friends had. *Neh*, she'd only visited her girlfriends and dreamed about finding a boy to walk out with. Some of her friends did that, and some took things too far. She stayed so sick, she could only take small amounts of any fun and games. She might not be the life of the party, but she did know rude when she saw it. This Tanner person wasn't pleasant at all.

"Here we are," he said a few minutes later.

The cart whizzed on so quickly, she'd forgotten to chat with him. Or maybe she didn't want to chat with him. Studying the rows of white cottages lined up along her *aenti*'s street, she loved how the palm trees swayed in the wind, and she enjoyed the beautiful blooming vines and flowers in each of the neat yards. The scent of a thousand blossoms assaulted her and the mild temperature felt so *wunderbar gut*. This town was like another world compared to the winter she had left. It was late February and still snowing there, while here flowers were already beginning to bloom.

"Aenti lives in a beautiful place," she said, almost to herself.

"Indeed, she does," Tanner replied, looking up at the lacy white porch posts and matching railings. "She keeps it clean and welcoming."

Eva did feel welcome now, knowing her *aenti* would soon greet her and get her away from this burly man.

Ignoring him, she took in the cottage. Two white rocking chairs sat on one side of the door; a small wicker table containing a small pot of orange flowers sat between them.

"I can't wait to see the rest," Eva said.

Tanner shook his head, his expression blank. "She loves her little *haus*. She has a tearoom in the back, for the tourists."

"You don't like tourists, ain't so?"

"Is it that obvious?"

"You seem to make it very clear, *ja*." Or maybe he just didn't like her, which made more sense. She was a Plain Jane, a sickly woman who'd missed out on love.

"I don't like people and that is so."

Giving him a shocked stare, she asked, "What made you that way? I've never heard of someone who doesn't like others."

He shrugged. "I don't like being around all the tourists, but I have to admit I make my living off their purchases."

"Then you should be grateful *Gott* gave you a business and people to buy things from you, ain't so?"

"I reckon I should at that," he said with a bit of humility.

Eva hopped off the cart and tried to grab her luggage, but Tanner did the same, their hands touching.

Feeling a tingle of warmth shooting up her arm, Eva tugged at the handle. "I have it. *Denke*."

Tanner didn't let go. "I can carry it in, Eva. I don't mind."

Eva held tight. "I wouldn't want to keep you from work."

"It's not a bother," he said in what could have been another annoying drawl. Then he took the suitcase and lifted it like a feather and started up the steps.

Eva followed, hurrying to catch up. She was about to give him a piece of her mind when the door flew open and Aenti Ramona came running down the stairs.

"Eva, you're here. *Kumm, kumm.* It's so *gut* to see you. Look how you've grown. You're so pretty. You'll be tanned and glowing before the week is out."

Tanner stoically carried her suitcase up the few steps to the porch, his stony face unreadable. But Aenti ignored that and hugged Eva tight. "I'm thinking you're hungry. Tanner, let's get my girl fed. You can join us."

"I need to get back—"

"Nonsense. I made a special meal. Meatloaf and mashed potatoes with peach pie for dessert. You'll stay."

Tanner's expression wavered between panic and the need to eat. "I guess I'm staying then," he said, not smiling at all.

Would it be such torment to be around her, Eva wondered.

And why should she care? She'd be gone sooner than later, and she'd probably never see Tanner what's-his-name again.

She hoped.

Chapter Two

"Now tell me how your *mamm* is doing," Aenti said while she poured iced tea into pretty goblets and served up chunks of meatloaf and creamy mashed potatoes along with steamed string beans.

"She is fine," Eva replied. "She fretted about me coming alone, but she refused to leave her work and friends, and she hated the idea of getting on a bus. I think she's afraid of everything in life."

Ramona nodded, her dark eyes full of understanding. "*Ech, vell.* Helen always was the cautious one, while I was the adventurous one. I do miss her though."

"And she misses you, but she enjoys sewing and keeping up with the doings of Campton Creek."

Aenti laughed at that. "I know it was hard for her to let you *kumm* here alone. I had to do some tall talking to persuade her. But I promised I'd look after you and that I shall do. I wish Helen would have *kumm,* but you and I will have a great time. And I thank Tanner here for picking you up at the bus station."

"Not a bother," Tanner said, his tight smile almost human. "I get this *wunderbar* meal, so it wasn't half bad going to the bus station."

Eva studied him while they waited for her *aenti* to sit down. He was tall and rugged looking, with hair the color of burnished straw. His eyes were interesting, topaz and ever changing, but she only glimpsed at him when he wasn't looking. She did not want that dour gaze to zoom in on her.

He had a neat beard, which meant he could be married. What woman would want such a rude and burly man anyway? He looked old enough to know better than to act like that. Maybe a few years older than her twenty-two years. Not her type, and already taken possibly. But then, she didn't really have a type. Alive and available might be her only requirements, but she wouldn't hold her breath on anything.

"Okay, now we can eat," Ramona said, smiling at them as her gaze bounced from one to the other with pride before she lowered her head to silently pray.

Eva did the same, praying she could make friends here and feel better, and hoping this man would stay away from her once he'd had a meal. He could get back on his strange cart and go back to whatever work he seemed so inclined to finish.

But when Eva lifted her head and caught his gaze on her, something like a streak of bright sunshine hit her soul.

He blinked and grabbed a biscuit at the same time she reached for one.

"Excuse me," he said, pulling his hand away.

Eva held to her biscuit and nodded, the warmth of his touch burning her fingers. "I'm hungry so I apologize."

"Oh, my. Eat up, you two," Ramona said. "And after you're settled in and rested, we can take a stroll. I can't wait for you to see the ocean, Eva. It's one of *Gott*'s greatest creations and a gift to all of us."

Eva wanted to shout that the man sitting across from her might think he filled that category of being a gift, too. But the woman who got stuck with him would not be gifted with his charm. She'd be in trouble.

Tanner ate his food in silence until Aenti asked, "How is little Becky?"

Then the man looked up and smiled for the first time since Eva had met him.

She almost choked on her green beans. He was quite good-looking when he smiled. Quickly, she took a sip of tea. Maybe he did have a loving wife after all. Maybe Becky got to see that smile a lot.

"Becky is Tanner's little daughter," Aenti explained. "She is eight years old and the cutest little thing."

So he did have a wife. Confused, Eva didn't ask. Things could be different down here and she didn't want to pry. "Maybe I'll get to meet her soon."

"I doubt that," Tanner said, then realized he'd said it. "I mean, she has lots of people looking after her while I work."

"Hard to pin down," Eva filled in, accepting the brush-off with a tad of regret. So… Becky didn't have a mother?

"*Ja*, hard to pin down." Then he lowered his head. "Her *mamm* died when Becky was a baby."

"Oh, I'm so sorry," Eva said, wishing she hadn't been too curious. Now she understood the beard and the gruffness. Poor man.

"*Denke.*" Tanner stopped eating and took a gulp of tea.

Something shifted in the air, but Eva couldn't put her finger on it. His words and actions reminded her of someone else she knew well.

Her mother.

Overly protective and distant, that's what Tanner was. Just like Mamm. And Eva wanted no part of anyone else who was that way. She'd come to Florida to take a break from her *mamm*'s protective, well-meaning misguided love. Eva had always been bold and curious, as her *mamm* pointed out. Reckless, Mamm would say. Too curious and caring for her own good.

Mamm had tried to reel her in, but Eva had a streak of adventure in her and this trip had resulted, ironically, from that streak and her constant health problems.

She'd avoid Tanner as much as possible, but she felt an instant bond to little Becky. But when she looked at him, he seemed confused and sad. He was a widower after all. He'd had to raise Becky on his own, just as Mamm had raised Eva on her own.

Eva ventured another glance at him. Tanner looked up, his bronze-colored eyes going dark. "Ramona knows everyone, so I'm sure you'll have plenty of friends soon."

"I hope to meet a lot of people here," she said, trying to smooth over the situation. "I want to explore all of Pinecraft."

"Oh, *gut*," Aenti said, "but that'll take only about an hour or so. We are a small community." Then she laughed. "You'll soon know everyone here and you'll see a lot of this one." She pointed to Tanner. "I help watch Becky at times."

Eva nodded, but she saw the dread in Tanner's eyes. And something else. Fear.

What was he so afraid of?

Tanner walked back into his shop and let out a long sigh. That had taken longer than he'd planned. He'd eaten too fast and now the spicy meatloaf was burning against his ribs. At least he'd made a fairly proper exit after dessert and some forced small talk with Ramona and her niece. Still not sure about Eva, he did like her pretty eyes and her shy nature. Shy until he'd acted like an idiot around her. Then she'd let him have it.

But he hoped Ramona wasn't trying to match him up again. The last few times she'd tried had not turned out so well. Disasters, that's what they'd been. Giggling girls, pushy mothers, stone-faced fathers. And so much food he'd had to give some of it away. He'd had enough for one season.

Ramona meant well, of course, but Tanner planned to stay single for a long, long time. He had Becky to consider after all.

"Daddi!" His daughter came running, her blue sneakers hitting the wooden floor with a squeak, her *kapp* ribbons flying out with a few strands of unruly strawberry blond curls fluttering along with them. Stopping to put her hands on her hips, she stared at him with deep blue eyes. "Where you been?"

Martha followed, shaking her head. "She just arrived from school a half hour ago. You'd think you'd been gone for months."

"It seems that way," he said, still rattled by all the feelings he'd experienced each time he looked at Eva Miller. Scooping Becky up, he held her close, the scent of milled soap and chocolate surrounding her. "Did you have your drink?"

Becky bobbed her head. "I did. Aenti Martha made it extra special 'cause I got a boo-boo on my knee."

"From running too fast up the street," Martha said. "I waited at the front door, so I saw her all the way home."

"Denke," he said as he lowered Becky down. "Okay, time to rest and go over your lessons."

"I don't have any lessons," Becky said. "I learned it all at school."

"You are a smart one," he replied as he watched her head to the play area he'd set up for her behind the big long front desk. "Now I must get back to work. James can't be left alone too much."

"'Cause you have customers?"

"I do. I have lots of orders to make special things for so many people."

"I luv you, Daed."

"I love you, too, Becky-boo."

Martha gave them both an indulgent smile. "James is delivering that small side table to Mrs. McCormick. She called asking about it."

Tanner nodded to Martha and then went back into his workshop, where the world went away and the quiet would take over.

The quiet of being lonely, of a tension that never left his mind, of always worrying and wondering and thinking of Deborah. His wife who'd died shortly after giving birth to Becky.

He'd loved Deborah for a long time, but she had planned to marry another man. A forbidden man. That had not worked out. So Tanner had confessed his love and Deborah had agreed because he was her only hope. They'd had a *gut* life, and she did love him, even if she had not been in love with him. But their time together was short and over before they could really grow close.

Then came Becky, without a mom. Him without a wife.

This workshop was his sanctuary and his life now. He created beautiful things from natural wood, and he'd even begun to create some pieces from recycled plastic, reusable vinyl, aged brocade and other materials. His work kept him calm and steady, while Becky reminded him of unconditional love.

It was enough. It had to be enough. He would never marry because he had to protect his daughter from the cruelty of the world.

When he heard her giggling in the front room, Tanner nodded and reaffirmed his reasons for this life.

He'd never marry again.

Even if his friend Ramona had a new prospect for him. Obviously, that's why she'd sent him to the bus stop when she could have easily walked there herself to receive Eva. He didn't want a new relationship.

Even if Eva turned out to be very pretty when she smiled.

Eva slept late the next day. Embarrassed when she saw the late hour, she hopped out of bed and hurriedly cleaned her room and freshened up in the tiny washroom connected to it. She put on a bright pink dress her *aenti* had made for her and tied a white apron over it. After putting her hair up in a neat bun, she grabbed her *kapp* and hurried into the small, dainty living room.

She found a note by the *kaffe* pot. "Had to go to the market. Back in a bit. I have Danish in the bread box." Then the next words encouraged her. "Go out and find a challenge, an adventure if you'd like. Just stay in our community where you are safe."

Eva poured herself some *kaffe* and grabbed a cheese Danish then went out on the wide front porch. The warm tropical breeze played through her hair and went on to dance around a set of butterfly-embossed wind chimes made of carved wood and held together by thick leather tethers. Unusual and pretty.

After their lunch yesterday, Aenti Ramona had taken

her on a short bus ride to see the ocean. When they approached the worn path down to the beach, Eva had taken off her blue flip-flops, another gift from her *aenti*.

"We like bright colors down here, Eva. It reminds us of sunshine and the beautiful ocean—gifts from *Gott*."

After she'd shyly dipped her toes in the crashing waves and saw all the colors of the water, Eva knew she'd never want to leave this place. The turquoise-and-green water made the prettiest sea lace, as Aenti called it, when it hit the shore.

"It's so beautiful," she'd told Ramona. "I can understand why you love it here."

"I do, indeed," Ramona had replied with a smile. "I met my husband, Steven, here and well, I couldn't leave him for some other woman to find."

Aenti loved to joke and laugh—the opposite of Eva's stoic *mamm*. Mamm was distant and quiet. She didn't like to get together for frolics or any type of celebrations. So birthdays and holidays had been simple and just the two of them most of the time. People would come to visit, but not that often.

Aenti Ramona probably had lots of friends. She'd said to find a challenge or an adventure, but Eva wasn't sure where to start.

Now as she sat here and enjoyed the strong brew and the *wunderbar gut* pastry, Eva did want to explore more. She wanted to learn to ride a bike and walk to the market where everyone here shopped. She'd heard of Yoder's Fresh Market, and she couldn't wait to see what she could find there. Eva liked to bake, and she aimed to do a lot of that. Maybe her *aenti* would let her learn, rather than discouraging her and shooing her out of the kitchen.

She was about to get up and go inside to find busywork, but a young woman came strolling up the white brick walkway.

"Gut daag," the woman said, waving.

"Hello," Eva replied, smiling. "My *aenti* is not here right now."

"Well, I came to see you," the woman, who looked a bit younger than Eva, replied. "I'm Teresa Stoltzfus. I saw Ramona at the market, and she told me you were here. I decided to *kumm* and meet you, and to *welkom* you to Pinecraft."

"How kind." Eva took in the light blue dress and Teresa's pretty organdy *kapp*. She envied Teresa's shiny brown hair, thinking how dull her own dirty blond hair must look. "*Kumm* and sit with me. I'm waiting on Ramona to get back so I can go exploring."

Teresa clapped her hands together. "She told me you might say that. I offered to be your guide. I know where all the *youngies* hang out."

"Oh, I've been through *rumspringa*," Eva explained, embarrassed.

Teresa sat down in the other rocking chair, her flower-embossed flip-flops snapping with the back and forth of the chair. "*Ech, vell,* so have I. The most boring part of my life."

"Really?" Eva sat up. "You don't like frolics and parties?"

"Oh, I liked them. Too much. But I came to my senses and didn't do anything I'd have to confess before the brethren, thankfully. But I do know some girls who did."

Eva gave her a doubtful glance. "So you like to gossip?"

"*Neh.* I don't repeat anything that could harm someone. But I do know a few things." Teresa's smile was infectious.

Teresa started giggling. "Oh, the look on your face. Of course, I don't gossip, and I know very little about any scandals around here. But I can tell you all about those who are friendly and those who are best left alone."

Eva thought of Tanner. *Neh*, she would not start off on the wrong foot by soliciting gossip on the man. Teresa had been kind enough to *kumm* and find her and befriend her, so she wouldn't jeopardize this budding relationship by asking questions about Tanner. After all, the man's secrets were none of her business.

Chapter Three

"So we have Phillippi Creek surrounding our community," Teresa explained the next day as they met to walk around again. "It's a pretty place with all kinds of wildlife, including alligators, and it's prone to flood now and then. So be aware. And we have Pinecraft Park where we go on picnics and walking trails. Bahia Vista is the main thoroughfare, so we try to avoid all the *Englisch* traffic coming and going."

Eva jumped each time a loud automobile shot by making pops that sounded like guns firing. She'd been here two full days now and the noise still scared her. So much happening.

"Backfiring," Teresa explained. "Vehicles are noisy things, ain't so?"

"Very much so," Eva agreed. "I'll never get used to this."

"It took me a while," Teresa said. "My folks moved here from Missouri and let me tell you—it was a big adjustment."

"Why did they decide to move here?" Eva asked, since she'd already told Teresa about her own health, the only reason she'd ever consider coming here. That and her need to escape for a while.

"My *daed* got a job offer to work on an *Englisch* horse farm not far from here. Some of the best horses in the world come from Florida, most racing horses. But my *daed* works with the quarter horses and draft horses. He does not condone gambling."

"That sounds like a *gut* job," Eva said as a seagull flew by, cawing at them. "Mamm and I have one old mare who can barely get us around. We walk most of the time."

"Hush, bird," Teresa teased. "We don't have any bread."

Eva laughed. "Ramona let me feed the gulls on the beach yesterday," she told Teresa. "They are so lovely, but she did warn me not to overfeed them."

"*Ja*, and they like to eat and then…well…leave their droppings behind."

"I saw that," Eva replied as they giggled and kept walking. Then she said, "I need to learn to ride a bike, but I want to walk more first. I haven't coughed much since I arrived, but I do tire easily."

"Let's go and find some food and you can rest," Teresa suggested. "You've seen most of the places the young folk hang out. We like the beach, too, of course."

"Do you swim in the water?" Eva asked, terror filling her heart. The ocean was beautiful but also ever changing and deep.

"We do, but I just splash in the waves. We wear our clothes for modesty's sake."

"That's *gut* to know," Eva replied. She'd seen some tourists in less clothing than a *bobbeli* newly born.

They came to a huge bulletin board that held color

fliers offering events to attend and help wanted signs. "What is this?"

"One of our ways of communicating about things. If there is a mud sale or festival, a post goes up here as well as in the local paper, which isn't much of a newspaper, just happenings around here. This is the best place to look for events, work and a place to live. And frolic or youth events. We'll want to look for those so I can introduce you to some of the fellows here."

"I doubt a fellow will notice me."

"What?" Teresa glanced at her. "You're pretty, Eva. You just need some fresh air and sunshine to rosy your cheeks. Your doctor was wise to send you here."

Fascinated, Eva read several of the posts and noted the help wanted ones. Then she read a flier next to an advertisement. "Is there a church here?"

Teresa studied the invite to a singing in a few days at the local church. "*Ja*, of course. It's an actual building since none of us have a large enough property to hold services. We have Mennonites here, too, so we share."

"A church building?" Eva shook her head. "So much to see and observe, to learn about."

Teresa took her arm. "So you like it here?"

"I do. It's exciting and different. And warm. I love that."

"It grows on you, the ocean, the warmth, the palms and flowers. All part of *Gott*'s world."

Eva smiled then spotted an ice cream shop. "Let's get some ice cream."

So far, she was certainly enjoying her vacation here. What would Mamm think?

The next day, taking the same route and full of ice cream and cookies, they were on their way back to Ramona's when Eva spotted a sign on a storefront. The same one she'd noticed on the bulletin board yesterday. Help Wanted. See Inside.

"I should get a job," she said. "Pay my way with Ramona and save up some to help Mamm."

Teresa glanced at the sign. "Do you want to work in a stuffy old shop where it's mostly wood and some accessories and clothes for the *Englisch*?"

"Does it bring stuffy old money?" she asked, smiling.

Teresa twisted her lips and finally nodded. "I suppose it does." Then she shrugged. "I work in one of the cafés here, just part-time, and I help your *aenti* as needed, too. I have two brothers to look after when my parents have to be away."

Eva studied the shop. "I see purses and bracelets and some clothing, even Amish clothing. It might be interesting."

"Then go in and find out," Teresa said. "This is where your *aenti*'s friend works. You should see. Want me to wait here?"

"Please," Eva said. "I shouldn't be a minute. Who would want to hire me anyway?"

Teresa waved her on and found a bench. "I'll be counting palm trees and bicycles."

Eva went inside the small shop, the scents of fresh-cut wood and lemon oil surrounding her. The driftwood pieces—tables, baskets, wall arts and candleholders—were impressive. Unlike anything she'd ever seen before. And the clothes were intriguing—some flashy and colorful made for *Englisch,* and a whole section of clothes for Amish, including all kinds of hats, sneakers and flip-flops. Along with some beautiful *kapps*.

"Good afternoon," a petite Amish woman said from behind the counter. "May I help you?"

Panic set in as Eva made her way toward the woman. What had she been thinking, coming in here? She never acted on impulse, but she did need to find something to do besides walk around all day. Maybe she should have discussed this with Ramona first.

The woman must have sensed her hesitation. "Do you need dresses or aprons?"

"I came about the job," Eva said on a squeak. Why was she so nervous? "I could use some part-time work."

The woman gave her a quick once-over. "Have you worked before?"

"*Ja*, in a hat shop back home in Campton Creek."

The woman gave her a kind smile. "I've heard of Campton Creek. We get visitors from there at times. *Welkom*. Okay. Let me get the owner. He'll be the one to interview you."

Eva bobbed her head. She'd hoped this kind woman might explain things to her. Maybe an older man owned the place, and this was his wife. He'd be understanding and give her this opportunity, she hoped.

The woman went to the door to the back and called out, "Tanner, you have someone interested in the position."

Tanner. Was he the Dawson in Dawson Department Store? Why hadn't she realized that when she'd seen that name on the big sign over the front door. That familiar name. Eva turned to flee. There was no way she could work for Tanner.

"Hello?"

Eva stopped, the one sharp word making her stiffen her spine. She pivoted. "Hello."

Tanner looked so surprised and full of dread, she almost laughed. But this was serious. She'd made a horrible mistake by coming in this place.

He walked toward her and crossed his arms over his broad chest. "You need a job?"

Eva held her hands together against her apron and glanced around to avoid looking at him. Then she finally faced him. "I thought I might find part-time work since I'll be here for a few months. I need to get home at the end of April."

"I see." He eyed her as if she were an ugly bug. "Are you sure? Have you ever held down a job?"

"I worked at the Bawell Hat Shop in Campton Creek, where I'm from. I helped out up front at times, but mostly I cleaned up the production floor where they make the hats."

She didn't tell him she'd had to quit because she got sick and Mamm refused to let her go back.

"I'll have to check there for verification."

"You can do that." But what if Mamm heard this news.

"You don't look too excited," he said, about to turn and go back to whatever he'd been doing. But he stopped and stared at her. "Any employee checks I do are to remain anonymous, if that makes you feel better."

It did, but now she felt like a criminal with a record. "That's fine. I have nothing to hide."

His eyes flared after that comment, like maybe he had a few things to hide himself. "Why do you want to work here?"

"I told you—I need the job. I can't let my *aenti* pay all my expenses while I'm here, and I want to save up so I can help my *mamm* when I return home. I'd just need work for two or three months."

"Still, you don't seem so sure."

"I'm sure about the work, but not so sure about working for you."

The woman who'd called him out to meet Eva snorted.

He gave his associate a sharp glance, followed by what could have been admiration. "I'm not a tough boss, am I, Martha?"

The woman behind the counter shot him a blank glance. "I've had worse."

"See, a roaring endorsement," he said, not even smiling.

"That's because I'm your cousin," Martha replied, giving Eva a nod. "We could use another young person in here, you know. James is a great worker, and he's loyal but in awe of you. You and I are old and cranky, I'm afraid. Another young person can be a breath of fresh air."

"I'm not doddering yet, and neither are you," he replied, that almost smile creeping along his handsome face. "I just don't know about this, Eva. I don't know you."

"Then never mind," she said, turning to leave. "It was a bad idea and too impulsive. I'll find work elsewhere."

After she heard what could have been a shove, Tanner appeared behind her. "Wait."

Eva turned to see Martha behind him, nodding at her and mouthing *Please*. With a grin.

Eva smiled, causing Tanner to look back at his cousin. "Martha, I mean, Martha *and I* would like to have you work here with us. If you want to do that, Martha will train you to work out front with the customers. Would that be suitable?"

Customers. She'd be around all sorts of people. What if she got sick again? What if Mamm found out?

What if you don't try?

That voice in her head, along with her *aenti*'s suggestion that she find a challenge or an adventure, caused Eva to stand tall. "I will check with Aenti Ramona and let you know tomorrow if that is okay. But I'm sure she will agree."

"That sounds fair," Martha said before Tanner could say a word. Martha handed her an application form that had appeared on the counter.

Shrugging, Tanner said, "*Ja*, that sounds fair. Since Martha already agreed." Then he added, "So you'll work part-time, mostly afternoons, help with customers, and also with unpacking inventory and keeping the work areas clean. And Eva, don't worry. You'll hardly see me. I prefer the back of the store much more than being up here."

He really didn't like people. She felt sorry for Martha, but Martha seemed content if not incorrigible. Eva liked her. Not so much the frowning man who stood waiting on her response.

"So, how does that sound?" Tanner asked, the question hanging in the air like a challenge.

Challenge accepted. Let the adventure begin.

"Me up here and you back there? That should work out great for both of us," she retorted, thinking she might not last a week.

And she had a feeling Tanner Dawson might be thinking the same thing.

Chapter Four

A few hours after reluctantly agreeing to hire Eva Miller, Tanner left the shop and walked the block to his house, where yet another female cousin watched after his eight-year-old daughter, Becky, while he worked. He never knew which of his three cousins he'd have since his relatives lived all around Pinecraft and the womenfolk took care of business while he tried to focus on Becky having a relative with her at all times when he couldn't be there. They made their charts and handed him a copy. He thanked them and made sure someone showed up, then gave them a big discount at the store. He was blessed to have a big family to help raise his child. So he tried not to complain. But then, he wasn't a talking man anyway. Tanner had learned at a young age to keep his thoughts to himself. He'd had a stuttering problem, growing up back in Ohio, but an *Englisch* doctor had helped him overcome that affliction.

Tanner glanced around, still amazed at the beauty of this community. Dr. Tatum always talked about how he came to Florida to fish and enjoy the fresh air and warmth. After Tanner had learned the craft of woodworking, the doctor had asked him to create a table out of some driftwood he'd found on one of his trips down here. Then the good doctor had mentioned Pinecraft.

An Amish community in Florida?

Tanner had become intrigued, but life had other plans for him at the time. He'd been in love with Deborah Cooper for most of his years. He'd planned to ask her to marry him and if she'd agreed, he'd planned to move to Pinecraft. Before he could ask her, Deborah had confided that she was in love with another man. Heartbroken, Tanner had left Ohio and come alone to Florida. A few weeks after he'd arrived, Deborah showed up at his door, needing help. She explained that the man she'd planned to run away with had been a rookie police officer. An *Englisch*. He'd been killed while serving a warrant. She was in trouble and unmarried.

Tanner did the only thing he could do. He married her.

Now he heard his sweet daughter's familiar squeal as she called out, "Daed, you're home!"

Becky ran down the steps of the small blue cottage they'd lived in since Tanner had arrived here a few years ago, her blue eyes, so like the color of their house, lighting up his world.

"Home I am, *liebling*," he said as he lifted her up in his arms. "I see Cousin Leah and you have been planting flowers again."

Colorful pots filled with yellow, pink and orange flowers of all shapes and varieties lined the wall of the porch, while black clumps of potting soil lay scattered all over the gray-planked floor, showing the evidence of their efforts.

"We worked hard," Becky said, her eyes bright with pride and joy, a smudge of dirt marked across one of her dimples. "I planted daisies and petunias and Leah said we'd have gardenias smelling so very *gut* when they bloom."

"Ah, gardenias," Tanner replied, grinning at Leah. "There is nothing quite like that sweet scent on a summer night."

"Leah says sometimes they make her sneeze."

Leah, eighteen and as pretty as Becky, nodded. "*Ja*, if I sniff too close. But their scent is nice floating on the night air along with the jasmine."

"*Denke,*" Tanner said to his younger cousin. "Do you have plans for the rest of your evening?"

Leah nodded, her brown eyes shining. "Jacob and I are attending a beach frolic. The weather is nice today, ain't so?"

"*Ja*," Tanner said, wishing he had more time to walk along the shore. "I might have to get out there soon."

Becky giggled. "Daed, you always say that, but you don't go to the beach with me."

Tanner saw Leah's eyebrows lifting. "She doesn't miss a thing," his cousin murmured as she started cleaning the porch. "Oh, Tanner, I hate to tell you this but I'm taking a job in the quilt shop down the street. I get to teach them all about quilting."

"That's good to hear. I know how you love making your quilts. But are you saying you can't help out anymore?"

"*Ja,*" she replied. "I'll be there most of my days so I'm afraid I can't be counted on to stay with Little Miss Butterfly."

"I don't want her to go," Becky said, giving Tanner her sad look. "But she promised she'd still visit me."

"I surely will," Leah said. "And I'll teach you to quilt, ain't so?"

"Ja." Becky smiled then, her mind fluttering like the insect he liked to call her.

Tanner put Becky down and touched a finger to her nose. "Help Leah clean up and then after supper, we'll bring out your bike and you can ride along the sidewalk. How is that?"

"Gut," she said on another squeal. "Not the beach, but *gut.*"

Tanner helped them sweep up and then waved Leah home to her large family. Glad that many of his relatives had moved here, too, Tanner still felt that old piercing in his heart. He loved having family around, but he knew he'd never have any more immediate family than his sweet Becky. The guilt of not spending enough time with her shadowed the pretty late afternoon like a cloud. He worked a lot, and that was a fact. But he did it for Becky. For her future and her security.

The burden of losing her mother when Becky had been born hung over him like a horsehair cloak, always irritating and bothersome. But he loved Becky, so he wore that cloak without complaint.

Most days.

Today had been a difficult day. Eva Miller had rubbed him the wrong way and now she'd be working with him. Or in his shop. He planned to avoid her like he avoided as many people as possible. But something about her had aggravated him like a gauntlet being thrown down.

Like a challenge he had to meet.

If only he could figure out what that challenge was supposed to be.

"Daed?"

Becky's hand tugging at his shirt brought him out of his thoughts. "I know, Butterfly. You're hungry, right?"

Becky nodded as she lifted her arms like a butterfly. "Well, *ja.* Leah made chicken potpie."

"Our favorite," he said as he guided her to the sink to wash up. "Help me get ice into the tea glasses and we'll sit out on the back porch and enjoy this fine weather."

"Okay," Becky said, heading toward the icebox. Florida Amish had two things most other communities didn't condone—electricity and indoor plumbing, both sparse but necessary since this community was on the edge of a big Florida city.

His *little maedal* was always smiling and happy. She'd been an easy *bobbeli* since the day she'd been born. Maybe her way of making up for not having a mother, but Becky rarely complained. If she got tired or fretful, she'd just grab her favorite flamingo-embossed quilt and her stuffed bunny rabbit and curl up in Tanner's lap.

He loved nothing more than holding Becky close until she fell asleep. She never asked much about her *mamm.* He'd told her early on that her *mamm* was with *Gott* now and would always watch over her. One day, he feared the whole truth would come out, so he had to protect Becky. Overprotect, according to his family members. Not his immediate family. His parents had not approved of Deborah, and they had not been happy when he announced he was moving to Florida. They rarely saw Becky these days.

But others in his family had been kind and understood his need to get away with the girl he loved. When they'd received word of Deborah's death, they'd showed up here in Pinecraft one by one, until half his kinfolk were now his neighbors. While the women of the family thought he needed a wife to balance things out, Tanner knew he had good reasons to be protective. And he would continue to watch out for his daughter as long as the Lord allowed him to live.

Now he grinned at her as they plated the still warm potpie and went out the open kitchen door to the screened back porch, a haven facing a little fenced-in yard full of queen palms, hibiscus bushes, gardenias and jasmine that covered the top of a trellis near the back fence. The early blooms hadn't started yet, but soon his yard would be a true garden. Not a bad view, and one that always made Tanner feel secure and at peace, if only for a few hours each day.

After they'd finished their supper, Becky obediently helped put away the leftovers and together, they did their evening ritual of washing and drying the dishes.

"Bike time," Becky called out as she hopped off her "dishwashing" stool and ran to the back porch.

"Bike time," Tanner echoed, smiling even though every muscle in his body ached. He would enjoy the gloaming with his *dochder*. Then tomorrow he'd get up and go through the same routine he had for years now. The sameness keeping him steady and secure.

Only tomorrow would be different. Tomorrow, Eva Miller would be working in his shop. And frowning at him with an unabashed disapproval. Well, he could frown with the best of them. Maybe if he out-frowned the woman, she'd avoid him.

He wanted that—he wanted her to avoid him, because he sure planned on staying away from her. He'd avoided every woman his nosey cousins had sent to him. He didn't want to ever be married again. The pain of watching Deborah die had almost done Tanner in forever. But holding little Becky had squelched that need to shut down and curl up in a ball. He was responsible for Becky.

He lived with that responsibility every day.

After he and Becky got the bike out onto the sidewalk, and Becky took off, spinning the bike's wheels, her bonnet strings flying out behind her, Tanner glanced ahead on the road to make sure no traffic was coming, and then he turned to make sure the sidewalk was clear.

And saw Eva Miller walking toward him with Teresa Stoltzfus, the two of them so involved in their conversation they only looked up when Becky called out, "Hey."

Then Eva jumped back and stood staring into Tanner's eyes, her smile turning to a frown. She'd brought her application back this morning. He'd barely glanced at it because Martha had a "*gut* feeling" about hiring Eva.

Now what? Should he introduce her to Becky?

He didn't need to. Becky never met a stranger.

Which scared Tanner more than dealing with Eva's frown.

The more people got to know Becky, the more dangerous things could become for her.

But Eva Miller didn't know that, and he prayed she never would.

Eva wanted the sidewalk to swallow her. She'd seen this man three times in the two days she'd been here. And one of those times, she'd asked him for a job.

Teresa held her arm. "Is that—"

"—Tanner Dawson. *Ja*, that's him. My new boss."

"He does not like women from what I've heard."

"I can vouch for that," Eva replied in a whisper.

"Hey," the little girl in front of them said again, her feet planted on the ground while she steadied her tiny bike. "I'm Becky."

Eva couldn't ignore that sweet smile or those big blue

eyes. The child was adorable. And her smile made up for the man's frown.

"I'm Eva," she said, leaning down to face Becky. "Is that your bike?"

"It's mine." Becky bobbed her head. "I have training wheels now, but one day I can ride without them, Daed says." She glanced back at Tanner. "Do you know my *daed*?"

Teresa snorted and covered her mouth with her hand.

Eva glanced at scowling Tanner Dawson. "*Ja*, I do know your *daed*. In fact, I will be working at his shop, starting tomorrow afternoon."

She shot Tanner what she hoped was a daring stare.

He strolled up, smelling like soap and sunshine, his gold-brown eyes and shaggy brown hair reminding her that he was handsome even if he did frown and scowl and act grumpy all the time.

"Becky, this is Eva," he said, motioning toward Eva as if she were an annoying bug. "And Teresa, right?"

"*Ja*," Teresa said. "I babysat Becky once when your cousin Trudy was sick."

"*Ech, vell*, I have a lot of cousins and *denke* for stepping in."

Teresa smiled big and looked goofy. Eva poked at her friend's ribs. "We were on our way home. Since it's getting late."

Becky glanced at the sky. "It's not sundown yet."

"*Neh*," Tanner said, "but some people have to get up early. So we should get on with your ride before your bedtime."

Becky wasn't finished visiting. "Eva, if you'll be working for my *daed*, we can visit. I like to *kumm* to the store and see Martha. She has cookies and *millich*."

"Does she now?" Eva asked, touching a finger to

Becky's nose. "And if I'm there, will you share your cookies and milk with me?"

"Ja," Becky said, giggling. "Martha says we are to share with friends. Are you my friend?"

Eva gave Tanner what she hoped was another daring stare. "I hope we can be friends. That depends on a lot of things, however."

Becky giggled again. "I think we can be *gut* friends. I like your smile."

Eva nodded, her eyes still on Tanner. "I like your smile, too." Then she mumbled, "And I'd like it if your *daed* smiled more."

Tanner's scowl only deepened. "Let's get home, Becky Butterfly. It's getting late. One time around the block and then bedtime."

Becky made a face but bobbed her head. "I can go fast."

"Not too fast," Eva cautioned. "You might have a fall."

Becky held to the bike's handles. "I'll be careful." Then she stopped, her feet dropping. "Can you be my babysitter, Eva? Our cousins won't mind."

Eva glanced at Tanner. The man couldn't have looked more uncomfortable if he'd been standing in an ant bed. And just to antagonize him a bit more, she said, "I'd love to sit with you sometime, Becky. I hope your *daed* will remember that."

Tanner's eyes narrowed. "Oh, I doubt I'll not be forgetting anything about you, Eva Miller."

Teresa held her hand to her mouth again, then she grabbed Eva by her apron and dragged her down the street.

While Eva could feel Tanner's eyes on her as they rounded the corner.

"I can't wait to see how he acts tomorrow," she told her friend.

"Better you facing him than me," Teresa retorted. "But for certain sure, he is a handsome but brooding man."

"That he is."

Eva didn't know if she was ready for that showdown.

Chapter Five

"I can't believe you," Aenti Ramona said, shaking her head, her smile wide. "Here what—four days—and about to go to work for Tanner Dawson, of all people."

"Ja," Eva replied, her stomach roiling in fear while she wished she hadn't been so impulsive and determined. "I can't believe it either. It happened so quickly."

Ramona's face twisted as if she'd swallowed a lemon. "Are you having doubts then?"

"Neh." Eva touched at her *kapp* for the tenth time. "I mean, *ja,* but I'm determined to try." Shrugging, she said, "Mamm would worry if she knew. I've already gotten a letter from her, which means she had to have written it even before I left. I hate not being honest with her."

"I see." Ramona took a sip of her favorite morning tea that she bought in bulk from Detwiler's Farm Market. "We don't want to keep things from my sister, but Helen has always been anxious. She frets about a hangnail."

Eva smiled and nodded. "You're right. She was a mess about me coming here, but she didn't want to leave her work, so I had to *kumm* alone." She giggled. "Make that, I had to persuade her to let me *kumm* alone."

Ramona lifted her head and straightened her back. "I might have had something to do with you being here without Helen, Eva. I suggested it would do you some *gut* to travel and see the world. By yourself."

Surprised, Eva studied her *aenti*. "But why?"

"I was afraid Helen would ruin your trip with all her worries. What if you'd gotten here and she'd made you stay inside or kept you on the porch, watching the world go by, same as she does back home, ain't so?"

Eva thought about that scenario. "I wouldn't have seen the ocean, or I might not have met Teresa. And for certain sure, she would not have allowed me to work at Dawson Department Store."

"*Ach, vell*, that is a fact," Ramona replied, her dainty sunflower-embossed teacup in her hand. "I love my sister, of course. But she has bad nerves, as our *mamm* used to say."

Eva could agree with that observation. "I've never understood it. I went along with her hovering for so long, trying to be mindful of respecting my *mamm*. I don't feel comfortable even saying this—but she really has held me back from some many things. I sat at home my whole *rumspringa*, while all my friends were out having frolics and fun."

Ramona took Eva's hand. "She was always fidgety and skittish, but when she lost your *daed*, she got even worse. That's why she protects you so much. She is afraid she'll lose you, too, I think."

"And I have been such a burden—always sick and coughing, sneezing, taking all kinds of medicines." Lowering her head, she said, "Mamm has given up a lot for me, and she always takes care of me. I shouldn't resent that."

"You might have allergies," Ramona said. "But my

sister tends to make her own diagnoses at times. She could have been wrong on some of yours, and yet she uses your sickness as a shield against the world."

Eva had never considered that. "I haven't felt as bad since I arrived here," she admitted. "I've been so busy sightseeing and now, I'll be working. But it's only three hours today. I hope I don't tire out, or worse, start coughing and sneezing all over the customers."

"I think you'll be fine," Ramona said. "Just drink your water and take your pills. That store is clean as a whistle, but Tanner does bring in clothing with a lot of dyes and such, and there could be sawdust and such floating in the air. You should let Martha know if you feel poorly, and then go outside for some fresh air when you can."

Eva gasped. "Tanner will fire me right off."

"Tanner has his own concerns," Ramona said. "His wife died during childbirth, and he's never fully recovered."

"Just like Mamm never getting over losing Daed," Eva said on a low whisper, the pain of what Tanner had been through hitting her heart like an arrow. "Becky?"

"*Ja.* Her *mamm*, Deborah, was a sweet woman, but she always seemed to be in another world. Sad at times and she didn't take very *gut* care of herself while she was with child. I don't think she liked living in Florida."

"That's awful," Eva replied, understanding Tanner a little better now. And her own mother, too. "I guess losing someone you love is never easy."

Ramona nodded. "I lost my Steven ten years ago and I still miss him every day. One reason I moved here. I couldn't take the cold weather without Steven there to hold me."

"I'm sorry," Eva said. "I'll be nice to Tanner, and I hope I don't get sick. He wouldn't like that."

"Tanner is a kind person, Eva. He just has a lot on his mind. He's overprotective, same as your *mamm*."

Eva didn't want to deal with that kind of pressure any more than she already had, but she surely didn't expect Tanner Dawson to protect her or even notice her. "I'll be aware. And Becky seems to be a spry adorable little thing."

"She is that, and she's the apple of his eye." Ramona nibbled on an oatmeal cookie, her expression serene and calm.

"I could tell that Becky is special when we saw them last night," Eva said. "Becky asked me if I could babysit her."

"Do tell."

She filled Ramona in on what had happened.

"He might take you up on the watching Becky," Ramona said. "After he lost his wife, his *aenti* and *onkel* moved their whole brood down here to help out. Two of the three girls and married now, but they still rotate taking care of Becky. Between all of them, Becky has plenty of people who love her, but sometimes he still has to find substitutes, since they all have families and jobs of their own."

"What about his parents?"

"They are still in Ohio. Old and ornery. They send Becky things, and he takes her up there to visit once a year." Ramona shook her head. "I hear they are not close with their son because he uprooted his life and moved down here with Deborah, but they tolerate each other. Maybe that's where he got his studious attitude."

"Studious? That's a *gut* word for it," Eva replied with

a chuckle. "He has a permanent frown. But last night he did smile when Becky was around."

Ramona's all-knowing gaze held Eva. "As I've said, she is his world. Be aware of that, too."

"Are you concerned for me, *Aenti?*"

"I'm concerned for your young heart, Eva."

Confused, Eva shook her head. "I think my heart is intact."

"And we must keep it that way," Ramona said with a soft smile.

Eva went through the day with nerves on edge and dread in her heart. Why had she agreed to work for the most brooding man she'd ever met? A man even her jovial *aenti* had warned her about.

Because she had something to prove—to herself and to Tanner Dawson. Now that she had some background information on him, she would try to be more considerate toward the man. But still…he would be a challenge. Had she been cloistered so long she now felt the need to take on a massive task, like David staring down Goliath?

She only hoped she didn't sneeze all over the pretty clothes she'd be showing off to tourists and Amish alike. Martha had told her she'd train her this first day and that she'd probably only work two or three days a week, and only a few hours per day.

"More than I've worked before," she mumbled as she helped Ramona set up a tea party for some *Englischers*.

That task distracted her for a few hours since she learned how many different tea choices Ramona served, along with fruit-infused water, fresh coffee and orange juice punch. Then she learned how to stack food onto the tiered serving plates and trays, sandwiches and sa-

vories on the bottom, scones and cream on the second
tier and finally to top it all off—dainty little petit fours
and colorful macarons sitting next to mini cheesecakes
and shortbread cookies. Once loaded with delectable
food choices, the white serving plates and trays etched
with pink-and-red roses around fluted edges made for
a beautiful display. Eva felt as if she'd fallen into a sto-
rybook world.

The six women who'd reserved the tearoom for their
private party loved the food and the tea. And they had
dressed for the occasion in floral sundresses and pretty
straw hats with ribbons around their brims. They smiled
and chatted like colorful birds while Ramona, Eva, and
the kitchen help did their jobs.

Eva stood in awe watching Ramona explain how she
brought the water to a soft boil in the sturdy white tea-
kettle. Then she heated the teapot with hot water and
poured that out before she placed the tea ball holding
measured teaspoons of a peach-flavored tea into the
warm pot, letting it steep for four minutes. Then Ramona served it with an elegant flair as she explained
the menu. The excited women called out compliments
while they picked from the sandwiches, scones and desserts layered on the serving plates.

Eva marveled at Ramona's efficiency and knowledge.
She loved the pretty mismatched fine china plates, cups
and saucers. Somehow, it all worked with the white
wicker furniture, fresh-cut flowers and lacy curtains in
the long dining room that looked more like a sunroom.

"That was so much fun," she told Ramona after
they'd had their own servings in the kitchen. "And this
food is *wunderbar*."

"I enjoy the tea parties," Ramona said. "They bring
in much-needed funding because I offer all kinds—

from birthday parties to wedding showers and anniversary celebrations. You name it—I can create a tea party for it. My home is paid for, and I can thank ladies in hats for helping me there."

Impressed, Eva patted Ramona's hand. "I'm glad I could help, since you won't accept any rent money from me."

"You are family, child." Ramona patted her hand back. "Now that we've rested and eaten, you will be full of energy so you can work hard at the department store."

Eva nodded and stood, then took a deep breath. "I hope I last longer than a day."

Ramona's smile shone in a smug way. "Oh, I believe you will last a long time. Tanner needs someone to ruffle his prickly feathers. And I believe you are just the girl for that."

"*Ja*, since I seem to have done that several times already."

She grabbed her tote bag and made sure her *kapp* was on straight, then headed out on foot toward Dawson's Department Store. All the while wondering how these next few hours would turn out.

Tanner listened to the chatter coming from the front of the shop. A busy day, and a different kind of day. Earlier, Martha had greeted the new hire with open arms.

"Eva, what a lovely pink dress. Did Ramona make that for you? It goes so well with your fair skin and those pretty blue-green eyes. Your hair looks like pure honey. The customers will love you, but you don't have to have your picture taken. They might ask because you are so pretty, but you can decline, of course."

Tanner had that image Martha had loudly described in his head now. Eva in a pretty pink dress, smiling at some flirty *Englisch* boy. Memories clouded his head like a true thunderstorm hovering in the sky, but as he always did, Tanner pushed the bitterness away. No point in remembering things he could never change.

Giggling from up front brought him back to the here and now and the big stump a customer had brought in today to be sawed and shaped into a table. It came from a beautiful cedar tree, but the tree man had salvaged almost all of it and his wife fancied a nice cedar table to place between two rocking chairs Tanner had made for them last year. They lived on Sarasota Bay in a large fancy two-storied home.

He needed to work.

He needed to check on things out front.

So with a grunt of a sigh, he opened the swinging door just to the left of the long counter and cash register and glanced about the aisles of the small department store.

Eva was folding beach towels. He had to smile at the way she held up each one of the oversize towels and studied whatever pattern was woven into the thick terry cloth. Palm trees and beach chairs on one. Flamingos, Becky's favorite, on another. A school of blue-and-yellow fish on yet another.

"Are you watching so you can learn how to fold towels?" Martha said from behind him, causing him to straighten his back and turn to glare at her.

"I'm watching the person you forced me to hire, to make sure she folds those towels correctly."

"*Ach, vell,* since when have you cared about beach towels?"

"I like beach towels. Becky has a whole collection."

"Because you never say no to that child."

"I discipline her as needed."

"Your Becky never is a bother. Is she coming here today since Katie has to work later at the bakery?"

"That is the plan," he said. "I'll fetch her from school and you and… Eva…can give her small tasks to keep her busy."

Why did saying Eva's name seem so intimate to him? He couldn't stop watching her and the awe on her pretty face as she discovered something new with each touch of her hand on material.

"She's *gut* at folding towels."

"What? Who?"

Martha's knowing smile only made him grumpy again. "Your *dochder*," she said. "And apparently Eva is doing a fine job, too."

He turned away so fast, he hit a rack full of shell necklaces his other cousin DeAnna had handmade. The whole thing rattled, tittered and fell over, causing both Martha and Eva to stare at him while he turned red and hastily tried to pick up the rack and the scattered necklaces.

"Let me do that," Eva said, kneeling beside him to reach for the jewelry, the scent of rose-fresh soap all around her.

"Neh." They both lifted their heads at the same time and came eye to eye with each other while Martha observed with a keen interest. Tanner looked into Eva's ocean-wide eyes and felt a strange burning in his heart. "I mean—I'll take care of this. I'm clumsy sometimes."

"Ja," Martha said as she pretended to be going over purchase tickets. "That's why we keep him in the back."

Eva startled laughing.

Tanner wanted to be mad, but he soon started laughing, too.

They laughed as they watched each other, and something so foreign happened inside Tanner's chest, he thought he might be having a heart attack.

He felt a burst of sheer joy as he stared at Eva.

"You smiled," she said, wiping at her laugh-filled eyes. "And laughed. You actually laughed."

"It happens," he replied, standing so quickly he got dizzy. Or maybe that was from staring at Eva for too long.

After placing the wire rack back onto the counter with a slide, he dropped the few necklaces he'd managed to retrieve next to it. "I... I...have to get back to work." Before he started stuttering like a shy youth.

He turned and rushed through the swinging door, its creaks and whines laughing at him as he went.

Martha was right. He should have stayed in the back.

Because now he had a really up-close image of Eva Miller imprinted in his head.

Chapter Six

She'd seen his eyes up close. His beautiful intense eyes. How was she supposed to work around the man now?

He laughed and her heart had jumped and shivered, and her pulse seemed to come alive with a longing she couldn't explain.

"How you doing over there?" Martha asked after Tanner had left.

Eva pivoted like a guilty child putting her hand in the cookie jar. She'd been staring at the back swinging door for a good five minutes.

Giving Martha a level glance, she said, "I'm fine. I... I'm learning the layout of the place."

"That door never really moves from that spot," Martha said, her hands on her hips. "But it does swing both ways."

"Hmph." Eva turned back to dusting the dishware display. "I sold a set of plastic cups."

"The *Englisch* love those convenient cups."

"And I've rearranged the beach towels."

"I saw. You did a fine job."

"I also sold two *kapps* to some *youngies*."

Martha chuckled. "You like to stay busy, for certain sure."

Eva glanced at that infuriating door again. "I don't want to lose my job the first day."

"Eva, if today is any indication, you are one of the best workers we've had. It gets downright boring in here at times, and then it gets busy, and we have to hurry up now. You've done well with both."

"If we don't count the necklaces falling to the floor."

"That was not your fault."

"I think it was. He wanted to get away from me and quick."

"He helped you straighten the jewelry rack, ain't so."

"*Ja*, because I was so frightened and—" She stopped before blurting out all the feelings she'd felt just being near Tanner.

"And you and Tanner had a *gut* laugh."

She smiled at that, remembering his laughter. "We did."

"So that's something. He rarely laughs."

Eva glanced at the clock. She had one more hour. Her afternoon had gone by quickly, and she wasn't too tired. She hadn't sneezed or coughed, thankfully.

"I like it here," she admitted to Martha, something in her heart wishing she could have a *gut* job like this back home.

"I think you will be just fine," Martha replied. "You got Tanner to laugh and that is worth having to pick up necklaces."

"*Ja.*" She grinned and went on with her dusting, her eyes drifting back to the big door. He was back there, working, creating, brooding, thinking.

What did he think about that spark of awareness they'd both felt? She'd never thought of that word *awareness* before. She'd never thought of a man like Tanner before.

Was it wrong of her to think of him now, to want to get to know him better, to want to understand him more?

She went about her work, straightening knickknacks, fixing bracelets that held dolphins, turtles and fish. Such a different world from hers.

The front doors burst open, and Becky came running in and skidded to a stop midway. "Eva, you're here."

Eva laughed. "I am. I work here now."

"With my *daed*?"

The smiling woman behind Becky took her time looking over Eva.

"I do work here. Just part-time, but I get to see you more."

"You like seeing me?"

"I do," Eva said, bending to give Becky a quick hug. "How were your studies today?"

"I'm learning arithmetic." Becky counted so fast, Eva lost the numbers in her head. "And reading. I like books."

"I like books, too," Eva replied.

The woman moved closer. "I'm Reba, Becky's cousin. She told me she had a new friend."

Eva nodded. "We met last night and now I get to see her again."

"I have to be quiet and stay out of the way," Becky said as she swayed back and forth, her green dress fluttering like leaves in the wind.

"I'm kind of doing the same thing," Eva admitted. "I don't want to get in trouble on my first day."

Reba said, "Why don't you go get your snack and maybe Eva can sit with you on the picnic table. I'm sure my cousin is allowing you to take breaks?"

Eva looked toward the door and then Martha. "I don't know if I get breaks."

"You do," Martha said, bobbing her head. "Get you some tea or water and sit with Becky. I'll let you know if we get busy."

Eva nodded, thirst and her aching feet winning out.

She only hoped the boss didn't notice her absence.

Tanner heard giggling again. He might be getting a headache from all the frolicking going on around his store. It had been this way since Eva had come on staff. She'd only been working for a few days, but she sure livened the place up. And Becky talked about her nonstop. They took breaks together out on the picnic table, all the while thinking he never noticed. He did notice and he should be annoyed, but he kind of liked the chatter. He also liked Becky having someone to talk to.

From here, he could see them out the window.

He looked up from a table he'd been commissioned to make with seashells and wood, to find his daughter eating ice cream at the picnic table out back. The bright blue umbrella was slanted so he couldn't see Eva's face. But he heard her voice.

"Hmm, *gut*, huh?"

"Ja," Becky said, bobbing her head, strands of hair slipping away from her *kapp*. "Thank you for taking me to get ice cream. I wish I could eat it for breakfast."

"That's a very *gut* idea," Eva agreed. "With chocolate syrup and a cherry on top."

"That would be the best breakfast," Becky responded with a slurp through her lips.

A bad influence, his new sales associate. He should go out there and fuss at her. He smiled before he could get a grip on holding back. He had to admit Eva Miller had brought some excitement into their lives. And all she did was stand there looking both stubborn and afraid in one facial expression, making him regret each word that came out of his mouth.

He heard chatter again when the neighborhood cat came running up, probably hoping he'd get some ice cream, too.

"That's Fancy," Becky said, pointing to the black-and-gray-striped cat. "He loves to be rubbed and he likes the kibbles Martha gives to him. Daed said Fancy doesn't need to eat ice cream, but he is allowed if it drops on the ground."

She demonstrated by letting her ice cream drip off her cone. "'Cause I make messes when it melts."

"Fancy is enjoying your mess."

"He is." Becky grinned and glanced back. "Daed will fuss."

Silence. Then, "Your *daed* is just training you up right because he loves you."

That statement stopped Tanner cold. How kind. Eva could have called him mean and harsh, but she'd told his daughter the truth. He did love Becky.

When he heard Becky's next words, he stilled, dropping the glue gun he'd been using to shape the shells along the table's edge.

"Do you have a *daed*?"

Another silence. Then Eva spoke so softly, he had to strain to hear through the open window. "I did. But he died when I was young. I don't really remember him, but my *mamm* always tells me he is here in my heart."

Tanner held tight, watching his daughter as she reached out her hand to touch Eva's arm. "Does he really live in your heart?"

"His spirit lives with me," Eva said. "Because he loved me. But *Gott*'s will was to take him to heaven."

Becky touched her own heart. "Then my *mamm* must live here some, too, ain't so?"

"I believe it is so," Eva replied, her words husky and low.

Tanner fisted his fingers, holding so tight to his emotions he could feel his fingernails burning impressions against his palms.

"Daed says she is in heaven," Becky replied, her ice cream melting and dripping on her hands. "I wish she could really be here. It's hard to fit all of her into my heart."

Tanner's eyes burned while his throat clogged with pain and grief. He watched as Eva leaned over toward Becky, her napkin wiping not at the ice cream dripping from his daughter's cone, but rather the tears from his daughter's eyes.

He inhaled a breath and put his hand to his mouth. Then he gripped the dusty counter, his grief followed with a rush of anger. Before he knew what had hit him, he marched out the open back door.

"Becky, time to come inside."

His daughter whirled as if she'd done something wrong. "Why?"

"Because I said it's time. I haven't had a *gut* visit with you today, and I wasn't told you'd gone with Eva to get ice cream."

Eva immediately starting clearing the table. She threw her own cup of ice cream in a nearby trash can and turned toward Becky. "Let's get you washed up. I need to go back to work."

Tanner walked close and took Becky's hand. "I'll take care of that. And yes, you should get back to work."

Eva's smile melted faster than the ice cream. "I will see you again soon, Becky."

Then she spun around, her head held high, and hurried back inside. Tanner watched her go, a shame washing over him. He'd been rude. But instead of telling Eva he was sorry, he turned to Becky. "You can read your books in the office, okay."

"Why can't I stay outside?" Becky asked. "I like talking to Eva."

"Eva has work to do and you need to rest before dinner."

Becky's pout almost made him cave, but fear and grief held him steady. "*Kumm*. I'll be done soon, and we'll go home and sit on the porch."

"I don't wanna," Becky said. But she followed him, her head down.

Tanner didn't want to cause his daughter any more tears and he didn't understand why he'd overreacted about her conversation with Eva Miller. Eva had lost her father at a young age, same as Becky had lost her *mamm*. Nothing wrong with how she'd handled the conversation, but it had riled him all the same. He wished he hadn't heard it, but he had, and his reaction showed him that he needed to stay away from Eva.

And so did his daughter.

Eva didn't know what she'd done wrong.

After she'd gone back inside and helped Martha sort some new inventory, Tanner had stayed in the back working while Becky sat quietly in the small office Martha had told her about.

"Becky sometimes reads there or takes a nap on the couch."

So Tanner had sent his daughter there to avoid Eva? It sure felt that way. She fretted, her mind whirling like a kite lost in the wind.

"Are you tired, Eva?"

She looked up from the colorful floral shirt she'd been unfolding to find Martha's kind gaze on her.

"*Neh*, just confused."

"You're doing great, but if you have more questions, I'll be happy to answer them."

"It's not that," Eva said, keeping her voice low. "I think I offended Tanner. Maybe I shouldn't have taken my breaks with Becky. Or maybe it's because I walked with her to get ice cream."

She told Martha what had happened, hoping Tanner couldn't hear since they were in the other corner of the store.

Martha listened and then nodded. "Hmm. It might not be the ice cream."

"Then what?" Eva tried to blink away her tears. "I'm afraid I'll be fired after a few days of work. He does not like me."

Martha took the shirt Eva held clutched to her chest. "It's not that, Eva. He's sensitive about Becky on all accounts. She wonders about her *mamm*, and he has a hard time explaining why she doesn't have a *mamm* like the other girls."

Eva glanced toward the swinging door. "Oh, no. He must have heard us talking about that. Becky asked me if I had a *daed* and I had to tell her that he died when I was young. Then she told me about her mother."

Martha nodded again. "That explains it then."

Eva shook her head. "Did I do wrong by sharing that with Becky? Is she too young to understand?"

"*Neh,*" Martha replied on a whisper. "It's just that Tanner is still tormented with grief, and he takes it hard when Becky brings up her *mamm*."

Eva glanced toward the door. "Should I go and explain?"

Martha glanced at the clock. "Your shift is over. You've done a great job this week. Go home and rest. This will pass."

"Do I still have a job?" she asked.

The swinging door flew open, and Tanner came walking toward them, his scowl back.

Eva's heart tried to burst out of her chest. "I guess I'll soon find out," she whispered. Had she ruined her first week at work?

Chapter Seven

Tanner glared at them, his blaze of anger fizzling out.

Eva gave him a firm gaze. "I'm sorry I took Becky to get ice cream without your permission, and that we discussed such personal things. I enjoyed working here, but you don't have to pay me for my short time. That's silly. I really did enjoy working with Martha and helping your customers. I'll find work somewhere else."

Martha let out a huff. "And yet another one scared and left."

Eva's eyes were so wide with fear and disappointment, Tanner felt lower than dirt. "No one is going anywhere," he said, his tone heavier than he'd planned. "You do work hard, and you deserve breaks. Next time, just tell me where you and Becky are going. I don't let her wander around, not with the busy main road and so many *Englisch* and tourists about."

Eva looked confused. "I'm not fired?"

Martha slapped a hand on her hip. "She's not fired?"

Tanner shook his head. "You are not fired. You are a big help to Martha."

"I am so thankful someone finally noticed that I do work hard, too," Martha said with a mock frown. "And that one of my best workers is going to stay." Glancing at Eva, she added, "I hope."

"I know you go above and beyond," Tanner explained. "And I also know that Eva stays busy, except for that ice cream break." He tried to smile, but his jaw muscles ached from gritting his teeth. To lighten that, he added, "Next time, invite me to go with Becky and you for ice cream."

Martha's gasp of surprise echoed over the empty store. "Well, I never."

"I have my moments," Tanner said. "I was rude today and I am sorry for that. Now let's get cleaned up and call it a day."

Then he turned and hurried back to his workshop, sweat popping out down his backbone, his palms moist with it. He didn't know which was worse, anger and bitterness, or grace and acceptance. Both made him extremely nervous.

Becky was up and drawing, her face twisted as she pressed her crayons against the drawing tablet he kept handy for her.

"What do you have there?" he asked, glancing at the colorful art.

"I drew Eva and me with ice cream," his daughter explained, pointing to the stick figures of her and Eva, complete with aprons and *kapps*.

"That is *gut* likeness," he said. Then he noticed another stick figure in the background. A man with an obvious frown, drawn with a straight line for lips. "And who might this be?"

Becky looked up and into his eyes, her expression torn between the truth and a sadness he couldn't erase. "That's you, Daed. I wish you weren't sad all the time.

I try to be the best daughter, but...are you sad because of me?"

Tanner's heart dropped as he kneeled in front of his sweet child. "I am never sad because of you," he tried to explain. "You are my sunshine and my joy, *liebling.*" Then he stood and lifted her into his arms. "*Daeds* get grumpy sometimes because we love so much, and we work so much. And we worry a lot."

"Martha says to worry is to waste your mind. She told me to always keep *gut* thoughts in my head." Then she gave Tanner an earnest stare. "Do you ever have *gut* thoughts in your head, Daed?"

Tanner smiled, but it felt awkward and bittersweet. "I have a great thought right now. Want to go to Yoder's and get a burger?"

"Can we do that, really?"

"I don't see why not. You have no sitter to cook for us tonight, so we're on our own. And I'm hungry."

"Me, too," she said. "Daed, you aren't sad anymore. You love hamburgers so much, ain't so?"

"I do, but I love you the most, little one." Tanner held her close and hugged her. "Never forget that my Becky Butterfly," he whispered.

Then his precocious daughter said, "We might ought to invite Eva because she thinks you're mad at her, too."

How should he handle that request?

In the end, it had already been handled. When they checked out front, Martha was locking up and Eva had already left.

Tanner's heart burned with regret in the same way Becky's mood shifted for a minute or two. But soon, they were both laughing and holding hands as they walked toward Yoder's, in the opposite direction of where Eva Miller was staying.

And yet, Tanner wished he could have invited Eva to supper with them. Then he decided it was best if he steered clear of her, the way he'd try to do all week. He'd have to be careful at work, and he'd watch out for Becky.

He couldn't allow his daughter to get too close to anyone besides family.

It was for her own sake, he told himself even if he wondered over and over if protecting Becky this much was the right thing to do. But what other choice did he have? No one could ever find out the truth about Becky's real father.

Eva was so tired when she got home, she almost didn't eat. Or maybe her nerves were getting the better of her.

"We only have leftover tea sandwiches," Ramona said as she laid the spread. "Egg salad and ham-and-turkey wraps. Will that do?"

"More than do," Eva said as she sank down. "I have to admit standing on my feet for three hours every day has worn me out."

"Then eat something, and I'll make you a soothing herbal tea to help you sleep."

Eva got up and washed her hands and face, her mind spinning with Tanner's anger and then his apologies. "I do not understand men sometimes, Aenti."

Ramona snorted while she placed the dainty leftovers on the pretty aqua-colored plates she used for every day. "*Ach*, *vell*, that is an age-old problem, I'm afraid. Men have their own way of doing things, even speaking. They can become very shy when they don't want to face a problem. It wonders me how they ever manage to fall in love and get married."

"And I am a problem, or it seems." Eva got out forks

and napkins. "This food is so *gut*, I hope I can get a bite or two in me."

"Let's take our plates out to the porch," Ramona suggested. "I love to hear the ocean breeze rustling through the palm trees. That fresh air is good for the soul."

Eva fixed a tray with their tea and plates, and Ramona carried it to the porch and placed it on a white table. They settled into the cushioned chairs and held their heads down for a silent prayer.

Eva prayed for her *mamm* back home, and she thanked *Gott* for allowing her to experience this beautiful world which was so different from anything she'd ever known. Then she asked the Lord to help her behave whenever she was around her boss. *Oh, and please, Lord, help Tanner Dawson have a better perspective.*

When she lifted her head, Ramona smiled over at her. "You had a lot to pray about, ain't so?"

"I did," Eva said. "I like it here. I'm glad I'm here to see the ocean and the palm trees and feel the warm wind on my face. I do feel better."

"That could die down once you get into a routine," Ramona replied, her eyes sad. "I had to make being a widow work for me so I could survive. I love holding my teas and I like baking, too. I earn a fair living here. But it's so *gut* to have someone to share these leftovers with, Eva."

Eva took Ramona's hand. "Mamm and I should have checked on you more and for certain sure visited you a lot more."

Ramona shook her head and took a sip of the tasty peach-chamomile tea. "Helen was never one for socializing. She prefers being by herself. We had to force her to the frolics and youth singings, and she paid no attention to *rumspringa*. Just found a boy to marry and made it happen."

Eva munched on some grapes she'd placed on the tray at the last minute. "She never talks about Daed. I know she misses him, same as you miss Onkel Steven. But you talk about everything, and you welcome everyone into your house."

"We are different, your *mamm* and me, but we both love you. Maybe since you are doing better and approve of my way of life, you can convince her to *kumm* for a visit."

"I could, but I'm thinking this is my *rumspringa*," Eva said with a grin. "Do I really want Mamm involved in that?"

Ramona laughed out loud. "Maybe not. Maybe later in the year, you can both return here, *ja*?"

"Wunderbar!"

Ramona finished off one of the tiny wraps and whispered, "But what would she think about you and Tanner?"

Surprised, Eva almost choked on her tea. "What about Tanner and me?"

"I think he's smitten," Ramona divulged, her eyes brimming with laughter. "He's never acted like this before."

"You mean, surly and brooding?" Eva shrugged. "I can't imagine why I'd bother him in a *gut* way, not when he seems to dislike me completely, and I seem to irritate him at every turn."

"That's another thing about men," Ramona explained. "Sometimes they say the opposite of what they are thinking or feeling. Sometimes, they get strong feelings, but they don't want to feel what they are feeling. So they act all mannish and puff up like a rooster and let loose a few loud blusterous rants or crows to hide their fears and worries."

Eva shook her head. "So you think Tanner is mad and scowls all the time because he likes me?"

"Could be," Ramona replied, sitting primly in her chair. "Just might be."

"I don't think so," Eva countered. "He came close to firing me because I didn't tell him I was taking Becky for ice cream. We could see the ice cream shop from his store. She wasn't in any danger. But mostly, he doesn't trust me. And... Becky and I talked about personal things today. About her *mamm* and my *daed*. That is what made him mad."

"He doesn't trust anyone," Ramona said, solemn now. "And he is overly protective as I've said. I don't know the story, but something happened between him and Becky's *mamm*. He was single and having a *gut* life and then Deborah showed up and soon they were married. Then she died so suddenly after Becky was born."

"Are you saying—"

"—I'm not saying anything because I don't know the truth, but he does and he's not only protecting his *dochder*, but himself too, I believe. I just don't know what happened."

Eva wasn't too innocent to understand the implications. Had Tanner wed Deborah out of love, or out of duty? Did he resent her death because she'd left him and their child alone?

"Do not judge him," Ramona said. "I shouldn't have mentioned this, but if you're to work with him, you need to understand his dark moods. It's been hard on him, raising Becky alone. And yet, he refuses to find another wife. And he's had lots of opportunities from the single women who flock to his shop with food and flirtations. He's immune to such."

Her *aenti* stopped and then glanced over at Eva. "However, he is not immune to a fresh-faced, pretty young woman who challenges him at every turn and seems to be able to hold her own with him and his temper. If you survived his mood today, Eva, there is a good reason for it. *Gott* is in the details, and I'm praying you will be a *gut* influence on Tanner and Becky."

"He did say to invite him next time I took Becky for ice cream," Eva said, not really believing what her *aenti* was suggesting.

Tanner had no interest in Eva. He had to be ten years older than her. Their personalities didn't match at all. He had a child. A beautiful little girl who needed a mother. Not a confused twenty-two-year old who'd skipped her *rumspringa* completely. Until now. Eva had been baptized, so technically she had to be done with running around.

But nothing said she couldn't at least have fun and enjoy her time here. But with Tanner? Never. Just never.

Ramona's eyes widened. Placing her teacup back on the table she said, "Well, I can tell you one thing for sure. He's never said those words to any other woman. You might consider taking him up on that offer."

Chapter Eight

Eva looked forward to her three hours of work over the next few days, but she sure dreaded seeing Tanner again. Her *aenti* had put silly notions in her head. Did Tanner really like her?

She'd managed to avoid him for two days now. He'd stayed in the workshop, and he'd made sure Becky went straight home with one of their cousins. He seemed intent on avoiding Eva, too. But Martha seemed to think he cared for Eva.

"I'll believe that when I see it," she mumbled as she hurried up the street to the shop. She didn't want to be late for the afternoon crowd. She'd studied up on beach fashions after finding some fancy magazines on a shelf in Ramona's private sitting room. Ramona had told her to take what she wanted since she'd already read them. Mamm would frown on that, but Eva considered it research in doing her job better.

She wanted to be the best employee possible, so she'd focus on that and not the handsome man who made her feel both scared and excited. What was wrong with her? She'd never experienced love like most of her friends. They'd walked out with all kinds of boys while she was usually at home sneezing or wheezing. Even now, she had some sniffles but for the most part, she was healthy. Except for her heart. It was changing and rearranging itself into a tizzy. And over a man who growled more than he talked. Was his grief that strong, that deep, so deep that he refused to be happy in life ever again?

Eva wasn't sure she wanted to fall in love if it made you feel like that. Mamm had chosen to never marry again, and she had not been happy. Now Tanner seemed the same way. Eva didn't want any part of a grieving man. But she did work for Tanner. Maybe she could ease his mind by doing her job. It would be a start. And she'd offer to help with Becky, to show him he could trust her. She'd ask his permission before she did anything with Becky, of course.

Having decided to take the high road and show Tanner some grace, she entered the cool shop and took a breath. Where was Martha?

Before she could call out, Tanner came through the swinging door with a scowl on his face. Not a *gut* start.

"Oh, you're here," he said. "Martha slipped on a rock and has sprained her left ankle. She has to rest over the weekend. So it's you and me today, Eva."

"You and me?" she echoed in a squeaky voice. "But I've only worked for a short while, and I haven't learned everything yet."

"You sold several items last week, and you rang up those items on the cash register, correct?"

"I did," she said on a gulp, her gaze hitting on him because his hair was wet, and he smelled like honey from the goat milk soap he kept on hand to wash off the sawdust and grime. "*Ja*, I did all that but…"

"But you don't want to work with *me*?"

"Do you want to work with *me*?"

Placing his arms across his chest, which only accentuated his broad shoulders and muscled biceps, he said, "I asked you first."

What could she say to that? And those biceps?

She said, "I don't want to upset you. Just tell me what to do."

Dropping his arms down again, he gave her a burly stare. "You know what to do, and you don't need to fret about me. I only work out here when I have to. If things get busy, just come to the door and call out to me. I'll help."

"Okay," she said. "Let me tidy up the shelves and see if we have any new shipments."

"Shipments only come on Thursday, so you are okay there."

She nodded, praying she wouldn't mess things up. "Anything else?"

"Becky will be here soon. But I have a cousin who'll meet her here and take her home."

Eva absorbed his words, her mind racing ahead to what might go wrong. He didn't want his daughter here with her. "All right. I will call you if I need you."

He gave her a quick nod, his mind probably on the project he'd left to explain things to her. "I appreciate this, Eva. It happens occasionally, but this week has been unusual."

"I guess I'll have my feet to the fire," she replied, smiling. Shaking inside.

"*Ja*, but you seem to take things in stride." He looked away and then back at her. "I'm sorry about the other day. I get cranky when I'm working, and I stay cranky a lot. Becky pointed that out to me. She was afraid she'd made me that way, that she's the one at fault."

"Oh, how could that sweetheart even think such a thing?"

His eyes went soft after hearing Eva's words. He had pretty eyes when they weren't all crunched in a frown. "She's never voiced it before, but I believe she thinks I'm mad at her. I don't want her to ever think that. And I'm not mad at you. It's just that—"

"I have interrupted your life?"

He grinned. "*Neh*, you have been a refreshing addition to our little world. I need to be thankful for that."

Eva blinked and lifted her head. "You're thankful… for me?"

He stood there a moment, as if he'd realized what he'd just admitted. "*Ja*, I am." He pivoted and left in a hurry. "Call if you need me."

He was grateful. That was all. Aenti had been wrong. Eva felt relief all mixed up with disappointment.

"I reckon thankful is a *gut* thing," she murmured as she dusted shelves and straightened clothes.

She could do this. She had a stool to sit on if she needed it, and water and some crackers to nibble if she got hungry. Martha had assured her that was all right to do. And she had caught on to things all week by shadowing Martha. The routine was a steady stream of tourists and locals, so she had to be prepared to get busy sometimes. She'd make sure nothing went wrong. So Tanner would continue being thankful to have her as an employee.

Everything was going wrong.

Eva glanced up at the line of tourists waiting to check out. A rush of teen girls had entered, giggling and whispering as they touched the clothes in the Amish section of the store.

"May I help you?" she'd asked a young woman wearing a crocheted cover-up over a very skimpy bathing suit.

"I don't think so," the teen had said loudly. Her friends giggled at that, their eyes hidden by dark sunglasses.

Eva nodded and stood watching them. They finally moved to the souvenirs but kept whispering. When their boyfriends came in, the girls whispered to their tanned, handsome friends.

They all glanced at Eva.

"I need a new pair of swim trunks," one of the boys called. Eva blushed and headed toward the swimwear section. "Right here. You can pick a size and we have a dressing room if you need it."

"I might." He chuckled. "Since you've probably never seen people like us much, huh? Wouldn't want to upset your stoic beliefs."

Eva wouldn't take the bait. "I see all kinds of people every day. Especially here."

They all laughed at that, while another customer stood waiting at the cash register. Then another one appeared.

"I must go and help these people," she explained. "I hope you find something you like."

Again, chuckles and snorts. Eva's skin burned and she wished she could hide in a closet. But she'd promised Tanner she could handle this. And she would.

Now she was struggling with ringing up merchandise and keeping her eyes on the group of six trying to vex her with all their might. Martha had warned her about shoplifters, so she had to be aware of that possibility, too.

Lord, give me strength, she prayed.

"I think you've overcharged me," the petite woman

waiting for a bag of seashells said. "I thought these were on sale."

Eva's backbone burned with sweat. Heat seemed to sear down her face and neck. "Of course. I'll need to ring this up again and void the first receipt."

The woman nodded and let out a sigh. "You need help here."

"I'm sorry," Eva replied, hoping she didn't burst into tears. She glanced at the swinging door, but she had no time to even ask for help. "Just let me get this corrected for you."

She fixed the receipt, but she didn't know how to void the first one. The woman paid cash, so she'd ask Tanner later how to clear the register.

The man behind the woman had two little kids with him. "Can you hurry? We'd like to get to the beach before the sun goes down."

"Ja," Eva said, taking the plastic sand buckets and shovels from the man. One fell down and clattered to the floor behind the register. "I'm so sorry."

Eva bent to pick it up and hit her head on the open cash register. A white-hot heat coursed from the pain in her head to her skin. She blinked to hide the pain and her burning eyes. She had to get things together.

The teenager who'd wanted to try on swim trunks called out, "Hey, girl, you don't have my size. Can you check in the back?"

More whispers and smirks.

"As soon as I'm finished here," she called out.

"I need you to do this now," the young man said, his voice rising. "We've been here for a while now. Hurry up."

Eva ignored him as she focused on ringing up the customer in front of her.

"So you don't know much English since you don't seem to understand me," the teenager shouted.

The man she'd just helped rolled his eyes. "She's busy, buddy. Back off."

"You stay out of this," the teen called.

Eva stood frozen as the two men shouted back and forth. Afraid they'd have a fight in front of the children, she came around the cash register and shouted. "Enough. I'll find your size after I'm finished here. Please."

She motioned to the frightened little boy and girl. "Please try to be patient in front of the *kinder.*"

"This store needs someone who can understand how things work," the teen said, stepping toward her. "And what's a *kinder* anyway?"

Eva braced herself for more harsh words.

The young man shoved several pairs of swimming trunks into her arms. "I've changed my mind."

Before Eva could grab the clothing, some of the trunks fell to the floor.

"Are you that incompetent?" the boy asked, his eyes dark with anger. "Really?"

The swinging door burst open, and Tanner came hurrying up the aisle. "What's your problem, son?"

The question came out in a low voice. But everyone heard it. The store went quiet. The older man with the children nodded and pushed them toward the front. "Thank you," he called out.

The teens stood there, smirking, disdain clear in their expressions. The girls huddled like wilting flowers while their boyfriends got fumed like fighting bulls.

"I asked a question," Tanner said. "How can we help you?"

"You need better service," the teenager said, but he'd lost the bravado he'd had earlier.

"And you need to learn some manners," Tanner replied. "How can *I* help you?"

"Never mind," the guy said, clearly confused and afraid now. "I'll find some new trunks in another store."

"Gut," Tanner replied. "I'm sorry we have nothing to offer you, but if you ever do come back, remember this. I expect you to be respectful of my staff. We work hard here, and we try to serve everyone. In return, we only ask that you respect us and our way of living. And I expect anyone talking to my staff to treat them with courtesy, even if there is a problem. We aim to please everyone, understand?"

"Whatever, man." The kid motioned and his followers fell in step behind him, the door chimes announcing their departure with what sounded like its own giggle.

Eva watched them leave then turned to Tanner, her breath coming in a rush. "I'm sorry."

Tanner frowned at her. "Are you all right? Did they upset you?"

Eva tried to speak, tried to swallow away the shame and pain, but she knew she wouldn't be able to say much. Grabbing at her throat, she said, "I need some air. I… I can't breathe."

Tanner grabbed her and rushed her out the back. "Go sit on the bench out back."

"The store," she managed, "not locked."

"I'll fix that. Sit and don't move. I'll hurry back."

She nodded and stumbled to the wooden picnic table. *Neh*, not now. Not now. She hadn't had a panic attack like this is such a long time.

Why now?

And why did it have to happen in front of Tanner?

Chapter Nine

Tanner rushed out the back door with a glass of water, his heart pounding like a mallet against his ribs. "Eva?"

She sat holding a hand to her throat, her eyes wide with fear as she tried to find air.

"What can I do?" he asked, unsure how to handle this. Then he remembered when he'd had to take CPR training in case something happened in the shop.

"Calm," he said. "I need to calm you down."

She bobbed her head, her eyes full of a plea for help.

"Water?" he asked as he kneeled in front of her.

She shook her head. Tanner placed the water glass on the table and then took her hands in his. "Eva, look at me. Take one deep breath."

She gazed at him and then struggled to get in a deep inhale.

"Now, let it out slowly, another, over and over," he said. "Breathe deep." He did the same and decided he needed this, too. "Now another, deep, deep breath and let it out."

She struggled to gain control, but finally her breathing went from frantic to slow and steady. Her expression held a trace of fear and shock, but her eyes were steady now, her pupils less dilated.

"Let's try one more," he coaxed. "Deep breath in and out. You're going to be all right. They are gone now and you're safe with me. Breathe deep and listen to me. You're safe. The air is fresh and clean, the creek is gurgling, and the ocean is only a few miles away. Keep focusing on that."

Eva nodded. "Water," she finally whispered.

Tanner held the glass. "Steady now. Just a sip."

She sipped, her hand over his as he held the glass. "More."

"Okay, but slowly." He tilted the small glass a bit more.

Eva took another sip then lifted her head. "Okay."

"Ja?" Tanner let out a long-held breath of his own. "You scared me. Does this happen often?"

Her relief turned to disappointment. "You're going to fire me, aren't you?" she said on a whisper that made its way into his heart and settled in.

"Why do you keep thinking that?"

"Because you are frowning, and you saw what happened. I made a mess of everything, and Martha says the customer is always right. I didn't please any of them today."

"Martha is not here, is she?" he asked, touched that Eva wanted to do a good job. "She is right to a point. We try to please our customers, but we do not put up with people who are being obnoxious and unreasonable and what I witnessed today was certainly that. You did nothing wrong."

Eva looked so shocked, he had to smile.

"Now you're laughing at me?"

"Neh," he said, frustration coloring the one word. Why did this woman seem to fray his nerves at every turn? "I'm not laughing at you. I… I think it's sweet that you care so much, is all."

She sank back against the bench and gave him a quizzical once-over. "So I'm sweet?"

Tanner couldn't seem to get himself out of the hole he'd dug himself into. "You are kind and a hard worker, Eva." Should he tell her he thought she was a sweet person, or would that make her angry again?

"So I'm not sweet, but capable."

Tanner grunted. "I liked it better when you couldn't talk much."

"So I talk too much?"

"*Neh*, I'm glad you can talk. You couldn't breathe a few moments ago."

She found the water and took a long drink. "I'm sorry. I want to do a good job. I like working here but these first few days have been hard. I'm afraid of doing something wrong and I'm leery of getting sick, and I'm afraid of you."

Tanner dropped back and lifted up to stand over her. "You do not need to be afraid of me. I will try to do better. I'm not used to someone like you."

"And who am I like?"

"You aren't like anyone I've ever known before, that is for certain sure. And yes, you are a sweet lady who has found a whole new world so different from the one you left and yet, you are so willing to do your part, to work and become a part of this community. You did a *gut* job today, Eva. Never doubt that."

She nodded and held her water glass in two hands. "I had a panic attack. I don't want to be sick, Tanner."

"What are you talking about? You just got too worked up and nervous, but you aren't sick. Are you?"

His thoughts went back to Deborah. She'd been depressed during her pregnancy, according to the doctor. Did all women get such anxieties, even the single ones?

Women were hard to understand. Tanner had managed to stay single because he was afraid of that kind of deep love again, and he was afraid of not being able to help the person he loved. He'd failed Deborah in every way. He never wanted to be that man again.

Eva must have seen the shock in his eyes. She stood and tried to get past him. "You don't want a frail, sickly worker."

He tugged her back. "Just explain this to me, please."

She glanced around like a lost doe wanting to jump the fence. "I have allergies and as a baby I had lung problems, a lot of respiratory infections. I'm better now, but sometimes I... I panic and that causes what happened today. It's not asthma but being anxious adds to my breathing problems."

"I had no idea," Tanner said. "Why didn't you tell me this up front?" He couldn't take secrets from another woman either. He would not abide that, and yet, this woman who appeared so innocent and naive, hadn't told him the truth. "I need to know if a worker has special needs."

"I have medication and I know how to deal with this most days," she said, her voice holding some fight now. "The panic attacks are not part of the sickness. They only happen when I'm tired or stressed—"

She stopped, put her head in one hand. "I should have never asked you for a job. I was rebellious and I wanted to take on a challenge. Maybe this challenge is just too much."

Tanner let out a sigh and sat down beside her. "I only ask that you're honest with me. Is there more I should know?"

"I'll tell you everything," she said. "It's not some dark, horrible secret."

Tanner felt the stab of that remark since he couldn't be completely honest with her, but he held his feelings inside and waited for her to continue.

"I've had pneumonia and severe bronchitis several times over the years and the last time, my doctor suggested I might need a change—the cold air is brutal on my lungs, and I get sick very easily if I'm chilled. The doctor suggested I *kumm* to Florida to visit my *aenti*." She stopped and hung her head. "I think even the doctor saw how my *mamm* hovered over me and protected me too much. She kept me inside even in the summer and fretted if I attended a youth event."

Lifting her head again, Eva faced him. "Doc told me I'd never get strong if I didn't have fresh air and sunshine. But I can see now, he wanted me to experience life—as long as I would be careful. But I haven't been careful here. I've been here over a week now and already I've panicked. Next, I'll probably become fatigued and get a sore throat and a cough. If Mamm finds out, I'll have to go home to the snow and the cold weather and her constant worrying. Since Daed died when I was young, I'm all she has. But I don't want to go back there. I sound selfish, but not yet, not yet."

Tanner's mind raced with a million reasons to tell her to go home and rest, and to let her know she didn't need to report to work again. But the forlorn look in her pretty eyes held him. He couldn't fire her, not when she'd tried so hard each day. Martha loved her and Eva had stood up to those bullying teens today.

"You don't have to go back yet," he finally said. "You can still work here—but no more than three hours at a time until you're steadier, and only when the weather is *gut*. No getting out in rain or storms."

She bobbed her head. *"Denke."*

Then he studied her. "I also have another idea that I think might work, too."

Surprised, Eva sat up straight. "What would that be?"

"How would you like to be Becky's companion as needed, which will be every day after school until school is out, and then it would be more hours. But that's only for the high summer, and you might not even be here then."

Eva let out a gasp. "You want me to tend to Becky?"

"If you'd like. You can help out with her here at the store and help Martha in a rush. You have the backyard here to enjoy and I can put up a covered patio for you two to do schoolwork and such. She needs help on her reading, and you'd be *gut* at that. I have lots of well-meaning cousins, but it's always complicated, having to pass Becky around so much. They mean well, but they're moving on to other jobs. She's getting older, and she needs stability."

"And you think I can give her that?"

Tanner wished he could show Eva just how much courage and spunk she truly had. He understood how her mother's hovering had almost ruined her, and she obviously felt that, to come all the way down here to get away for a while. She only needed responsibility and confidence, like most people. She could help Becky with that, too.

"I believe you are a *gut* influence on her, *ja*." He leaned close. "Despite the notorious ice cream incident."

She smiled at that. "I am sorry."

"Not your fault. I learned from it. I realized I've been coddling Becky and that needs to stop. You'd be a big help in that since you understand what being coddled means, ain't so?"

Eva smiled and shook her head. "You are always a surprise, Tanner."

"So are you, Eva," he replied, smiling back. "So are you."

Then he asked, "Well, do we have a deal?"

Eva waved bye to Tanner and Becky. Once Becky had arrived at the shop, Tanner decided they'd shut down early. So they hastily cleaned up and he showed Eva how to void a sale so the register receipt would match up.

"You're not walking home," he'd told Eva. "I'll bring the cart around."

Before Eva could protest, Becky clapped her hands. "Riding in the cart is fun, Eva. Have you tried it?"

"I have," Eva told her as she exchanged a speaking look with Tanner. "I had my first ride when your *daed* picked me up at the bus station a few days ago. It's different from riding a horse."

Becky giggled. "A horse doesn't have wheels. But Daed takes me to the riding stables, and I get to ride the ponies. He says that's how Amish get around up north."

"Your *daed* is correct. I'm glad he is teaching you the traditions we have in Pennsylvania."

Tanner came and stood with them. "Before I get the cart, Becky, I need to ask you something."

"Am I in trouble?" Becky asked, her eyes wide.

"*Neh*, this is a great thing," Tanner said, glancing at Eva. "How would you like it if Eva spends more time with you after school?"

Becky's squeal pierced the air. "I'd love that."

Tanner covered his ears and grinned. "Then we will discuss it a bit more when we get home."

"Is Eva coming with us?"

Eva intervened after seeing the doubt in Tanner's

eyes. "*Neh*, I am tired and my *aenti* is expecting me for supper. But she did say we might visit the ocean this weekend. Maybe you can tag along if it's okay with your *daed*."

"Can we, Daed?" Becky said, smiling. "You can *kumm* with us, ain't so?"

"I don't think—"

"You promised we'd go to the beach soon."

Tanner gave Eva a helpless shrug. "What can I say? I did promise that. If Eva doesn't mind."

Eva had readily agreed on Becky's behalf, but now as she waved to them she wasn't sure how she felt about being with Tanner at the beach all day. Becky had her heart set on it, and Eva couldn't turn her down. Eva would have Ramona as a chaperone, and she'd be careful about staying warm and dry, and away from Tanner. Surely she'd be fine. It would be nice to watch Becky's reaction to the beautiful sea. And Tanner's, too, at that.

When she reached the porch, she turned to see them rounding the corner back toward their house. And she had to wonder—had she agreed to spend the day with them because of Becky's request, or did she really want Tanner to be there with them?

"A little of both," she decided, smiling despite her doubts. "Just a little of both."

Chapter Ten

Saturday turned out to be a beautiful day. The temperature was in the seventies, a surprise Eva liked this early in the year. Back home, it was still winter. Here it seemed summer stayed all the time. Would she one day get tired of that if she lived here year-round? Right now, she didn't think so.

After she'd told Ramona that Tanner and Becky would meet them at the bus stop, her *aenti* clapped with delight. "Tanner is for certain sure changing his tune of not going to the beach."

"Doesn't he like it?" Eva had asked. Who wouldn't like a day near the amazing ocean?

"I think he has bad memories of the beach," Ramona had replied. "But that's his story to tell, not mine."

Eva itched to hear the whole story about his marriage to Deborah, but she would not be nosy. Tanner would tell her if he wanted her to know. Today she planned to relax and enjoy being near the sea. She'd survived working and now she could go back next week knowing she would be more involved with Becky and with the shop. Tanner had weekend workers in today and the shop was closed on Sundays.

Eva would be so happy to help with Becky. She'd always loved children, but Mamm would tell her she might not be able to have any of her own, what with her being as weak as a kitten at times. That stung even now, but Eva would do her best to help this one child who'd lost her mother.

As she and Ramona bustled around, packing lunch and remembering sunscreen and towels, Eva hummed a little tune.

"Remember you are to call your *mamm* before we leave for the beach," Ramona reminded her. Eva had received a letter from Mamm yesterday, stating she'd be waiting at the phone booth at nine in the morning.

"I won't forget," Eva replied. Mamm would not be happy if she missed the phone call. Checking the clock, she hurried to the front room where Ramona kept what she called a landline phone for business.

Eva tried to practice what she'd say to her overly protective mother. *Lord, let me say the right things. I don't want to upset Mamm, and I love her dearly. But I don't want to be rushed home just yet. Your will, Lord.*

After her silent prayer, she dialed the phone booth number.

And waited. The phone rang and rang. Had she gotten the time confused?

Nine in the morning—Eastern Time. That's what the letter had stated.

She hung up and then tried again.

"Eva?"

Relief washed over Eva. "Mamm, is that you?"

"Well, who else were you expecting?"

"I'm sorry. I tried once and you didn't answer."

"I only just got here. A goat was in my bean patch, and

I had to shoo him away. That infernal neighbor Moses Kemp doesn't watch over his animals."

Eva smiled. This was an ongoing feud. "Moses hasn't fixed his fences yet?"

"*Neh*, and the more I complain, the more he refuses. I think I need to have one of the bishops go and talk to the man. He is stubborn."

"And you're not?"

"Child, are you being rude to your *mamm*? Has my scatterbrained sister been teaching you to talk to me like that?"

"*Neh*," Eva quickly said. "I was only teasing. I know how Moses can be." She'd always thought Moses had a crush on her *mamm*, but maybe that was just Eva's imagination running wild again. The man was tall and willowy but had the strength of an ox. While Mamm was petite and stout and had the stubbornness of a mule. They clashed. A lot.

"Enough about Moses," Mamm said, her tone stern. "Tell me how your visit is going? Are you well? You sound tired. Are you ready to give up this nonsense and come home where you belong?"

Eva held her sigh. "I'm having fun. I've been busy. We are going to the beach today—"

"*Neh*, you will not. You are not a *gut* swimmer."

"If you'd allowed me to be taught—"

"I didn't want you wading in that dangerous creek, Eva. You know how I feel about that. And you will not go to the beach and the ocean. Do I need to speak to my sister?"

"Mamm, you told me to enjoy myself. I've had one quick glance at the ocean and today, Aenti Ramona and some friends will be with me. I don't intend to get in the water. I just want to have a picnic on the shore."

"A picnic on the shore. Aren't you the high and mighty one now!"

Eva didn't want to have another panic attack before they left. She would not let her well-meaning mother ruin this day. "I will be fine. Mamm, I'm twenty-two. You told me I needed to get out more, but yet when I try you want to hold me back."

"I have not held you back from taking this far-fetched trip to Florida. I hear things, you know. That community is not what we need, Eva. You should *kumm* home sooner than later."

Eva swallowed and closed her eyes, asking for patience. "I will be fine. I'll write you a letter tonight and tell you all about it."

When she saw Ramona motioning to her, she said, "I need to go, Mamm. I love you and please don't worry about me."

"Eva?"

"I love you. Aenti says hello."

"Send me a letter." Mamm hung up before Eva had to. So like her mother to get in the last word.

Ramona shook her head. "She wants you home, ain't so?"

"Very much so," Eva admitted. "And she demanded me to stay away from the beach. I know as a child, I was taught to obey her, but is it wrong to tell her no now that I'm an adult?"

Ramona came to Eva and took her hands in hers. "You are an adult, but your *mamm* doesn't want to let go, Eva. She went through the horrible trauma of losing your *daed*, and she has watched over you in fear that she'll lose you. This is a big step for both of you. You are allowed to be you, made as *Gott* made you. As long as you are not disrespectful and acting out, you are fine. And you are here with me. Does she think I'd lead you astray?"

"I think maybe," Eva admitted. "But you are a *gut* influence on me. I've found work that I like and people I like being with. Is that so wrong?"

"*Neh, liebling*, that is not wrong at all." Ramona let go of her hands. "Now let's get our baskets and towels. We'll wait on the porch for Tanner and Becky to give us a ride to the bus station."

"And I invited Teresa," Eva said. "I forgot to tell Mamm I have a new friend."

"I'm guessing you forgot to tell her all about your job and Tanner and Becky, too," Aenti said with a smile.

"I ran out of time," Eva replied with her own smile. She didn't like keeping things from her mother, but how else was she supposed to become independent and healthy.

She stopped after they were on the porch. "Aenti, do you think Mamm's over-caring ways have made me worse or better?"

"You seem better here, Eva. You've only had a few sniffles and you continue to be happy. I can't speak for your *mamm*, but smothering is just as bad on someone's health as ignoring their needs completely, you understand. Either way, you don't win."

"I'm not trying to win," Eva replied. "I only want to be myself, well and healthy and enjoying the life *Gott* gave me. I will need to pray on this. A lot."

"That is the best way to solve our problems," Ramona said. "Let *Gott's* will be done."

"*Ja,*" Eva replied. "I only hope He shows me the right path."

"He always does, dear," Ramona replied as she waved to the approaching cart. "He always does."

* * *

Tanner took in the air and the water, his face turned to the sun. He hadn't been to Siesta Key in years. Too long. They'd enjoyed their sandwiches and chips, and he'd walked with Becky along the shore searching for shells while Eva and Teresa trailed behind, laughing. Ramona sat by the picnic table they'd claimed once they'd gotten off the bus.

But now that he was sitting on a towel alone, watching his daughter frolicking with Eva and Teresa, memories crashed all around him, tugging at him in the same way as a rogue wave could take him under.

He couldn't avoid his memories forever. He had Becky to consider. Spending more time with her had to be a priority and he'd tried. But he had work to do and a business to run.

Maybe Eva could help with both Becky and the business now that he'd gone and given her extra duties. To help her and Becky? Or so he'd have her around more?

Neh. That was ridiculous.

But as he watched her now, chasing Becky along the shore, her light blue skirt flying out around her legs, he had to smile. Becky had taken to Eva in a strong way. Maybe he had, too. She got him all flustered; he knew that. And when he was flustered, he tended to be brusque and rude.

I'm working on that, too, Lord.

He didn't want to think of Deborah, but she would always be in his heart. He'd loved her and she'd tried to love him. But she mourned for another man, a man lost to her forever. And before Becky had been born, Deborah had often left Tanner to take the bus to the beach. She'd walk the shores alone, her mind far, far away. Somehow, in her grief she'd lost her mind, too.

Depression, the doctors told him. She'd get over it once the baby came. And if not, they could help her. Only she never got that chance. Sometimes, he thought his beautiful wife had hung on as long as she could—just until the baby had been born.

Laughter brought Tanner out of his dark memories. He had to be careful. He could never love like that again and he had to focus all his love on his daughter. *His daughter.*

Teresa rushed by with a beach ball. "I can't keep up with little Becky." She laughed and then tossed the ball back toward Becky.

Becky giggled as she chased the ball. But the wind picked up the light-weight plastic and sent it into the water.

Becky headed after it.

Eva called out and started running.

Tanner jumped up from his towel and hurried toward the water.

"Becky?"

A wave hit his daughter right in the face, taking her under.

Eva ran in after Becky, her hands grabbing for the girl's wet clothing. She pulled Becky up, both of them sputtering and coughing.

Teresa and Ramona both stood at the edge of the water, watching, their hands gripping each other.

Tanner grabbed Becky into his arms and then reached out for Eva. She tried to grab his hand, but another wave crested and hit her, causing her to lose her balance. She went down.

"Eva?" Ramona called. "Eva?"

Tanner handed Becky off to Teresa after he made sure she was safe and hurried back into the water to grab Eva up with both hands. Then he lifted her into his arms and carried her to the blankets they'd spread for their picnic.

"Eva? Are you all right?" Ramona called out, wringing her hands.

Eva coughed and sputtered but nodded her head.

Tanner checked on Becky and then stared down at Eva as he settled her onto the towel. "Are you sure?"

Eva's eyes, so wide and so like the ocean, held him there, her fear as strong as the tide, but her heart as open as the vast sea. Tanner stared back, his mind telling him to stop, his heart begging him to hold on. Until he let go and fell back to put his hands over his knees. His heart pumped out of exertion and fear, but also with a great need to hold Eva in his arms.

"Daed, I got wet," Becky said, running toward him. Then she pointed. "My ball is gone away."

Tanner glanced out at the water and watched the red-and-yellow-striped ball floating along the waves, too far out now to retrieve. It might wash up on the beach again, but it wouldn't be here in this spot. And no matter, he wouldn't be around to see it. Coming here had been a huge mistake. He could have lost Becky. And Eva.

"We need to get everyone home and dry," he said, standing too quickly. "Let's pack up."

"We didn't eat our cookies yet," Becky said, a pout on her lips. "I want my beach ball."

"We have plenty of beach toys at the shop," Tanner said.

"We can have cookies later," Ramona replied, concern wrinkling her face. "We don't want to get a bad sunburn."

Becky's disappointment mirrored Eva's. "I'm sorry,"

she said, coughing. "I should have been watching Becky more carefully."

Teresa handed her a clean towel and some water.

"*Neh*, I should be the one watching her," he retorted as he tossed things in one of the baskets. "I've been far too distracted lately."

Then he stalked off toward the bus stop. "If we hurry, we can grab the next bus back to Pinecraft."

He didn't miss the way Eva stared after him, her pout almost as pronounced as Becky's.

But he had to stop his feelings for her, somehow.

And how in the world could he do that now, after he'd practically begged her to spend more time in his world?

Chapter Eleven

"It's just a sniffle," Eva told Ramona the next day. "I coughed a lot and then I got chilled. I'm fine."

Ramona gave her a thermometer. "Just need to check. My sister will skin me alive if I let you get sick."

"I can't be sick," Eva protested before she let Ramona jab the thermometer under her tongue.

"I know. You're Becky's new nanny."

Eva bobbed her head yes. How could she have been so irresponsible? But she had to get to Becky in the water. Now she was embarrassed and afraid to ever go near water again.

She waited, tapping her sneakers against the wooden floor of the kitchen, her heart galloping ahead with fear and worry. Why couldn't she let go and give it all over to the Lord? Just being here was a sign from above, wasn't it? Or had this come about because of her stubborn need to be able to breathe on her own, to learn on her own and to make her own mistakes.

Well, she'd certainly done that yesterday, but she had to step out in order to find her footing. Before it was too late for her to find her own life. She'd go back to the water, and she'd be careful next time. Now that she knew the power of the ocean, she could stand strong against the current.

But the current rushing through her heart might be the one to bring her down next time. Each day brought new challenges and new strengths. Eva could handle whatever came. Why hadn't she learned all of this sooner?

Maybe because her beloved mother had fretted over her only child since the day she'd been born. Mamm hadn't been able to have other children. She'd preferred staying a widow to remarrying. So she doted on Eva.

A bit too much.

Ramona removed the thermometer. "Normal. That is a relief."

"I told you," Eva replied. "We don't have church today, and I'll rest until time to go and meet Becky at the store tomorrow. I'll drink tea with lemon and honey." She pointed to a packet on the table. "I have cough drops and sinus medicine that I brought with me."

Ramona took a sip of her tea. "You seem prepared. But even if it's only a cold, it could get worse with you."

"I hope not." Eva wanted to prove she was better now and that she could overcome any sickness.

Except the one piercing her heart. She'd seen how fearful Tanner had become when Becky went into the waves. She'd experienced the same terror, her reaction causing her to go in after Becky. But she'd also seen the resignation and regret in Tanner's stormy eyes. He'd not been happy about both of them chasing a beach ball into the lapping surf.

"Of course, Tanner might have changed his mind about me," she said, realizing she'd spoken that thought out loud.

Ramona brought her a cup of hot tea and a blueberry scone. "I think Tanner will get over what happened. It could have gone badly but we were all there and he got to both of you quickly."

"He won't soon forget what happened, even if it wasn't anyone's fault. He's so like Mamm."

Ramona gave her a curious stare. "Do you have feelings for Tanner?"

Eva blinked and gulped her tea. "I didn't like him at all, but now I understand him. He loves his little girl."

"But he is overly protective?"

"*Ja*, you see that, too?"

"I've said as much," Ramona replied, her forest green dress pretty against her white apron. The dress matched her eyes. But the look in her eyes reminded Eva of Mamm. Worry.

"I think Tanner cares for you, Eva. But I need to warn you—he won't follow through. He pushes women away faster than slapping at flies. He is afraid to open his heart to anyone except his child."

Eva broke off a chunk of her scone. The lemon-flavored icing tickled at her throat, but it tasted great. After chewing, she looked over at her *aenti*. "I care about Tanner and Becky. I feel for their grief. But I don't expect anything else. He's older than me, and he's set in his ways. He loves his work, and he is a *wunderbar* artist. He makes beautiful things out of driftwood. Wood that's just slipped away from the tide, as he says. He just needs someone to help with Becky. His nearby family members have been amazing, but he wants a more settled routine and schedule for her. I can help with that."

Ramona lowered her head and gazed at Eva. "But you might be going home soon."

"I could stay longer than I'd planned. Maybe?"

"Maybe?" Ramona smiled. "Are you considering doing that?"

"Would I be in your way if I did?"

"Neh," her *aenti* said, touching her hand. "You have made me so happy. I have someone to fuss over, but I also know you came here to spread your wings."

Eva stopped eating, wiped her fingers on a cotton napkin, then took Ramona's hand in hers. "You've been so kind, and here I am going on and on when you are probably just as lonely as Mamm at times, ain't so?"

Ramona's eyes misted. "I will never bear children. The doctors told me that long ago. After Steven died, I gathered friends around me, and I created a business that required me to stay busy. By inviting others into my home each week, I don't have time to be lonely. But there are days—"

A knock at the door caused Ramona to jump up and wipe her eyes on her apron. "See what I mean? No time to pity myself. Who could that be this early in the morning?"

Eva drained her tea and cleared away the dishes, her mind on anything she could do to help Ramona. Her *aenti* needed someone, just like Eva and Mamm needed someone. But now Eva's heart was torn between home and staying here in Pinecraft.

She turned from the view of blue jays and sparrows fighting over the bird feeder to find Tanner standing at the kitchen door.

Her heart did the same thing it always did when she was near him. It danced. "Tanner? Why are you here so early?"

But she knew why. He'd *kumm* to tell her he'd changed his mind about their agreement.

* * *

Tanner noticed it right away.

Something was off with Eva.

"I came to see how you are, after what happened yesterday. But I can see you're not well."

She touched her *kapp* and pushed a sprig of hair off her face. "Do I look that bad?"

"You look tired and pale." He glanced at the tea and the cough drops, thinking even so she was still a pretty woman. "Are you sick?"

"I am a sickly person, Tanner. I'll be okay. Just tell me why you came and get it over with."

Ramona had somehow disappeared. Surprised at Eva's bad mood, Tanner sat down across the breakfast table from her. "I'm here because I'm concerned, and I want to apologize."

"You have no reason to apologize," Eva said, her shoulders high now, her gaze direct. "I should have been watching Becky with a keen eye."

"I should have done the same," he replied. "She's my responsibility. But she doesn't understand the ocean can be dangerous. I plan to give her swimming lessons, but some fears go deeper than that."

Eva studied him with that blue-green color so like the sea shimmering in her gaze. "If you've changed your mind about me, I'd understand."

Tanner had to wonder why the girl always feared the worst in life. Could be, she'd never experienced much of life, being isolated and protected by her misguided mother. But she'd hit on the truth this time. He wasn't sure he should be near her or allow her to be with Becky every day. And that wasn't because of what had happened on the beach. It was more about what was going on inside his head and heart. But he also had to protect Becky at all costs.

But then, that would make him a lot like her mother. Was he being unreasonable in trying to protect Becky from the ugliness of the world? Or was he being unfair to himself and Becky by not reaching out to the world? To Eva. Well, he'd already done that, and he should regret it. But here he was, sitting before her, asking forgiveness.

"I don't understand."

"From that frown on your face, I think I'm right," Eva said, bringing him out of his revelation. "You're finally going to fire me. I lasted almost two weeks in the store and almost a whole day with Becky. I'm a failure at everything."

She started coughing, then stood to leave the room.

Tanner caught her by the arm and gently pulled her back. "Once and for all, I am not firing you. But I am concerned that in trying to please me, you are overdoing things."

Eva held her hand to her lips, her gaze rippling like a stormy ocean. "Overdoing?"

After taking a sip of water from a small glass she'd left on the counter, she shook her head. "I love overdoing, Tanner. I've never had any opportunities to do most of the things I've done this last week. I'm amazed and in awe of the ocean, that much water always moving and changing. Back home, I'm not able to help with the *kinder*. I haven't done much of anything except help Mamm cook and clean, weave and knit, and plant what little we can provide for ourselves. I made *kapps* and bonnets, and I sewed napkins and towels and placemats to have spending money. But I rarely got to go shopping. I told Mamm I'd like to follow the doctor's advice and see if it might help me to feel better. I knew I could afford the bus fare because I'm frugal with my savings."

She took a deep breath, coughed again, then looked out the window. "And I do feel better. Maybe my body isn't healing as much as I'd like, but my heart and my mind are feeling ever so much better. You think I'm overdoing, but Tanner, I've only begun to catch up. So this has nothing to do with wanting to please you, although I do want to work hard and take care of Becky. Being here, taking a job, agreeing to help you out with Becky, those are tasks I am capable of and want to take on. Do you understand me?"

Tanner stood at least a foot taller than Eva, but right now he stood in awe of her. She had such a courageous spirit hidden beneath that frail exterior. She took his breath away.

"Tanner, do you understand me?"

Tanner nodded and then he started laughing. He couldn't help it. She made him laugh. "*Ja*, Eva, I for certain sure understand you."

She might have stomped her foot, but Tanner couldn't take his eyes off her rosy cheeks. "But you find me funny?"

"I find you…intriguing," he admitted. "I do believe you are discovering your own heart, and I need to trust your heart and mine, and *Gott*'s will." He shook his head. "I'm not laughing at you, Eva. I'm laughing because you are brave and sure, where I am doubtful and distracted. I want you to be okay. I want you to be completely sure. I want to see you smiling and well."

She lifted her chin in defiance. "I will be fine, Tanner. And if I'm not fine, you have no cause to worry. Unlike Becky, I am not your responsibility."

"*Neh*, but you are a friend, and I will watch over

you as any friend should. I'll see you tomorrow afternoon then."

"Gut," she said, surprise in her voice.

"Gut," Tanner echoed. Despite his reservations, he wanted Eva to stick around for as long as she wanted. He'd keep watch, but he wouldn't let his heart get involved. *Neh*, not at all.

Chapter Twelve

Eva decided she'd walk to work today. Her cough had died down and she'd slept better last night. No tossing and turning, no fretting about losing a job she shouldn't even have. Tanner wanted to be her friend, and she made him laugh. She had to accept that, and she wanted the same. He was nice when he laughed. Even more, she wanted to be of help to Becky. Eva had never known her father, and Becky would never know her mother.

They could be a great comfort to each other.

"Eva?"

She turned at the corner and saw Teresa hurrying toward her. Waving, she called out. "Hello."

"How are you?" Teresa asked, hurrying toward Eva. "Ramona told me you had a cough."

"It's mostly calmed down now," she said as her friend fell into step with her. "I'm much better today. I suppose I'm not used to seawater."

"That salt water—not *gut*. And the bright sun can make you feel tired and dehydrated." Teresa pushed at a palm bush hanging over the sidewalk. "I'm to the market for some eggs and butter. Mamm wants to make a pound cake for my *daed*'s birthday tomorrow. You're invited, by the way."

Eva looped her arm with Teresa's. "I'd love that. I can see your home and you can show me this river you're always talking about."

"Phillippi Creek," Teresa reminded her. "A beautiful, tropical place, and just as dangerous as the sea. It tends to flood in storms, but bald eagles and osprey love it there."

"I'll stay away from the water."

"Gut," Teresa said as they reached Dawson Department Store. "And you'd be wise to watch for the snakes and gators, and the single men who'll be at the frolic."

She gave Eva a mischievous grin and then let go of Eva's arm and waved. "I must hurry."

"I should, too," Eva replied as she returned Teresa's wave, and decided to ignore that comment about single men. Eva wasn't interested in meeting any new men, and she sure didn't want to come across snakes and alligators.

But she liked Teresa and wondered if having a sister would have made a difference in her life. Another thing she'd missed out on.

"We are to be what you see us to be, Lord," she murmured as she entered the big store. And she was just an average plain girl who'd probably never find her true love.

She'd have to live with that. Meantime, she had a job, and she would start her new task—watching out for Becky after school each day.

Becky would be dropped off by some of the older scholars, and then Eva would leave the floor unless she was needed as backup. It should work nicely since standing around with nothing to do wasn't her idea of working. But she would help with checking the inventory and anything else needed. She could hang clothes, straighten merchandise and dust with Becky nearby. She'd teach Becky these chores. Amish children learned young to do their chores.

She opened the door to the cool inside of the shop and waved to Martha. Martha always had a ready smile and a jovial attitude. She seemed to let Tanner's many moods slide right off her. Eva could do that, too, with time and practice.

Time and practice. How much time did she have if she couldn't stay here?

"How is your foot?" she asked Martha.

"Much better. I've been propping it up with a stool when I can."

"I'm here now," Eva said. "You can rest as much as you need."

"You look so serious," Martha said after Eva had put away her tote bag and turned to face her.

"I was thinking about all I want to do," she admitted. "And how long I might be able to stay here."

Martha eyed the tote bag. "Are you moving in, then?"

"Not here in the store. Here in Pinecraft." Eva grinned and laughed. "Ramona sent cookies and a thermos of fresh lemonade. For the picnic Becky and I will have once Becky arrives. But she sent enough for most of the community."

"I don't mind a cookie and lemonade when I take a break," Martha said. "Ramona makes the best snick-erdoodles."

"Then you are going to be very happy," Eva replied.

The swinging doors to the workshop swayed and Tanner came up the aisle between the souvenir refrigerator magnets and the beach towels. "What's all the fuss about?"

Eva checked him for frowns. When she found none,

she nodded. "Ramona sent provisions since you work us so hard."

Tanner's gaze moved over Eva, but when he saw the smile creeping up her face, he shook his head. "Martha, your sarcasm is wearing off on our helper."

The doorbells jingled and Martha gingerly hurried to the front to greet two Amish women. Soon they were laughing and chattering about the mild winter and spring approaching.

Eva didn't want to think about that yet.

"So you're better?" Tanner asked, his tone unusually quiet, his eyes unusually inquisitive.

"I'm much better. Just a little tickle. It happens."

"I don't want you to be sick, Eva."

She stood up straight. "I'm fit to work."

He glanced over her again, making her skin become warm. Too warm. "You do have your color back. And your *kapp* is on straight."

"Is it? I seem to always have something out of place."

"You look nice," he replied with an almost frown.

To silence the awkward feelings, Eva said, "I'll just straighten the T-shirts while I wait for Becky. She should be here soon."

"She'll enjoy the lemonade and cookies," Tanner said.

"Were you listening to Martha and me, then?"

"I heard cookies and lemonade," he said with a shrug. "That caught my attention."

"That and your need to check on me and make sure I'm able?"

"You look able," he said, turning to go back to his work. "I have several pieces to carve, so I will be in the back most of the afternoon."

"I will see you later then," Eva replied, working to

keep her voice neutral. Even she knew not to bother Tanner when he was whittling and carving. He had the heart of a true artist.

She glanced around at the candleholders he'd fashioned out of driftwood, and the tables he'd made from cypress, cedar and walnut.

The swinging doors moved again, causing Eva to glance back.

Tanner returned to stand by her.

Nervous and highly aware of his nearness, she asked, "Did you forget something?"

"*Neh*, I thought I heard Becky, but I see she's not here yet. What are you doing?"

"Studying your work so I can be knowledgeable if anyone asks about an item."

A moment ticked by. "What do you think?"

"I think you are a *wunderbar gut* carver, Tanner."

"It started with an *Englisch* doctor back home," he explained. "He came down here to fish and hunt and once he brought home this huge driftwood log and asked me to shape it into a table. It reminded me of a turtle, so I worked it into a side table shaped like a huge turtle, and I had enough of the same wood left to put the legs on it."

"That sounds incredible. And cute."

"The doctor's wife loved it." He shrugged. "When Doc told me about Pinecraft, I knew I wanted to live here one day."

"And now you're here."

"*Ja*, but I didn't come down here for a while. I planned to marry and stay in Ohio. That changed, however."

Eva didn't ask how or why. She wanted him to tell her of his own accord.

"I only got serious about woodworking after...after Deborah died. We got married here, and while she was with child, she used to bring home driftwood and put it all over the house. After she passed, I picked up a knife and started whittling. I made some animal shapes that Becky still has to this day."

Eva didn't speak. Tanner rarely talked this much and had never talked to her about Deborah. Eva only touched the carving of a dolphin lifting out of the ocean. Made from washed-up wood.

Tanner shook his hat off and rearranged his wavy hair. "One day when I was walking the shore alone, I found a large piece of driftwood and remembering the table I'd made for the doc, I shaped it into a fish. I hung it right there over the cash register, not to sell, but just to display. But I got such a high offer, I sold it on the spot."

Eva smiled at that. "So that's how you got started."

Martha and the two other Amish women chattered away over the available dresses and other Amish clothing. They made merry music in the background while Eva waited to hear more from Tanner.

"*Ja*, I've been doing this almost as long as Becky's been here with me. The store was functioning when I bought it from an *Englisch*—an older man who only wanted to retire to fishing. He named a fair price, and I needed something to do. I couldn't go home to Ohio." With a nod, he added, "I guess it turned out best that Becky and I stayed here. She's safe here."

He stopped, glanced around, then turned to head back to his refuge. Eva stood staring after him, the small dolphin carving still in her hand.

He hadn't told her much of a personal nature, but she'd sure picked up on some cues. He and Deborah had married down here, and Deborah had looked for driftwood while she was pregnant with Becky. Tanner couldn't go back to Ohio.

Why was that? To protect Becky. Or to protect her *mamm*'s reputation? Or perhaps to protect himself and the how and why of what had happened between Tanner and Deborah.

Eva wanted to know, of course. But she also knew she'd have to bide her time. Because, after having told her all of this, Tanner would make it a point to avoid her. She was beginning to see the patterns of his moods. And she was beginning to understand more and more that he had some sort of secret reason for wanting to protect his child. An obvious secret, but one any man would take on. Because of love.

Could Eva accept that? For now, she had to. She'd be gone soon and none of this wouldn't matter to anyone.

Except her and Tanner.

Tanner tried to focus on the bowl he'd created from a cedar log. He'd shaved and curved the wood with a gouge chisel and a tough hook knife. He wanted to bring out the grain. He planned to stain it a rich but light ginger so the yellow veins could show through. This was a biscuit bowl, but he had enough cedar to make several dough bowls. Always popular. The wood had been treated and prepared, but cedar didn't need much to get any bugs out of it. It contained a natural repellent.

Checking the clock, Tanner began to pull the blue finger tape off his hands. His work was precise, and he used a lot of sharp objects, so he wore the tape most days.

Tomorrow he'd start on the dough bowls.

Martha and her sisters would pour scented soy candle wax into some of the smaller dough bowls. They had several favorite fragrances that brought return customers—

lilac, honeysuckle, gardenia and lemon were well loved. Vanilla was always a safe choice.

He thought of Eva and her allergies and upper respiratory problems. When they made the fresh candles, he'd need to warn her to stay away. He knew some preferred unscented candles, so he'd tell Martha to consider making some of those, too.

Maybe he'd make Eva a special dough bowl and have Martha create a light peppermint or eucalyptus scent to help Eva's sinuses.

And why did he keep thinking of this woman?

Because he'd liked her the first time he'd seen her. He could admit that now, even though he'd fought it from the beginning.

And now that he was getting to know her, he liked her even more. But he needed to keep his distance. No good could come with them being more than friends. He'd only make her miserable, the same way Deborah had been miserable.

But Deborah had been in love with another man.

"Daed?"

Tanner hurried to clean his chisels and knives so he could place them in their protective leather holder. "I'll be right there," he called to Becky.

But the door swung open before he could leave the workshop and in marched Becky with Eva behind her.

"I tried to keep her out," Eva said, her eyes moving around his sanctuary. "But she wanted to tell you something important."

Tanner lifted Becky up into his arms. "What is it, *liebling*?"

Becky giggled. "You smell like wood. The *gut* wood."

"Cedar," he explained. "I made this bowl today."

"That's pretty," Eva said as she inched closer. "And it does smell so nice."

"I have more," he said, giving her a quick tour. "I plan to make a lot of bowls. They sell like hotcakes."

Becky giggled again. "I like hotcakes."

"What news do you have?" he asked, smiling as he placed her back on the sawdust-covered floor.

Becky swayed, her hands holding her light pink skirt out. "I'm learning to sing so well, teacher asked me to do a solo at the end-of-school program."

Tanner glanced at Eva. Her smile brightened the room almost as much as Becky's did. "That will be something," he said, already worrying about Becky being the center of attention in a room full of people. "I can't wait to see you do that."

Becky turned to Eva. "He said yes. He never says yes."

His daughter was correct there. Distracted, he'd promised her something he normally wouldn't allow. But how could he tell her no now?

Chapter Thirteen

When Eva and Ramona arrived at Teresa's house the next day, it looked like the whole community had come to celebrate Isaac Stoltzfus's birthday.

"Isaac is popular here," Ramona pointed out. "Since their house is near Pinecraft Park where everyone plays shuffleboard, he sets up a concession stand—popcorn, sodas, lemonade and a freezer full of ice cream bars—right in his front yard. Snacks to feed people who love watching the friendly competitions. He gives the proceeds to the church, so we can help those in need in our community."

"How thoughtful." Eva smiled. "I hope Teresa made a big cake."

"I'm sure she did, but we all bring food," Ramona said. "There is a women's shuffleboard competition on some nights. You should sign up. You'd have fun."

"I don't know how to play," Eva admitted, glancing around. "Maybe Teresa can teach me."

"Well, *ja*. And you need to meet more people your age. We have several eligible young men around here."

Why was everyone trying to fix her love life?

"*Denke*," she said. She wouldn't be rude to her *aenti*.

Get up to 4
FREE FABULOUS BOOKS
in your welcome box!

To thank you for being a loyal reader we'd like to send you up to 4 FREE BOOKS, absolutely free when you try the Harlequin Reader Service.

Just write "YES" on the Loyal Reader Voucher and we'll send you your welcome box with 2 free books from each series you choose plus free mystery gifts! Each welcome box is worth over $20.

Try **Love Inspired® Romance Larger-Print** and get 2 books and fall in love with inspirational romances that take you on an uplifting journey of faith, forgiveness and hope.

Try **Love Inspired® Suspense Larger-Print** and get 2 books where courage and optimism unite in stories of faith and love in the face of danger.

Or **TRY BOTH** and get 2 books from each series!

Your welcome box is completely free, even the shipping! If you continue with your subscription, you can look forward to curated monthly shipments of brand-new books from your selected series, always at a discount off the cover price! Plus you can cancel any time.

So don't miss out, return your Loyal Readers Voucher today to get your Free Welcome Box.

Pam Powers

LOYAL READER
FREE BOOKS VOUCHER
WELCOME BOX

YES! I Love Reading, please send me a welcome box with up to 4 FREE BOOKS and Free Mystery Gifts from the series I select.

Just write in "YES" on the dotted line below then return this card today and we'll send your welcome box asap!

YES

Which do you prefer?

☐ **Love Inspired®**
Romance
Larger-Print
122/322 IDL GRET

☐ **Love Inspired®**
Suspense
Larger-Print
107/307 IDL GRET

☐ **BOTH**
122/322 & 107/307
IDL GRE5

FIRST NAME	LAST NAME

ADDRESS

APT.#	CITY

STATE/PROV.	ZIP/POSTAL CODE

EMAIL ☐ Please check this box if you would like to receive newsletters and promotional emails from Harlequin Enterprises ULC and its affiliates. You can unsubscribe anytime.

LI/LIS-622-LR_LRV22

"I'll look forward to meeting everyone and maybe I can try shuffleboard."

As they entered the park and found the Stoltzfus group gathered around several picnic tables across from their home, Ramona laughed and nodded toward the group. "Maybe he can teach you."

Eva's gaze followed Ramona's. Tanner Dawson.

Tanner turned as if she'd called his name and spotted them. Nodding and smiling, he broke away from the group of men he'd been huddled with and came to help them with the ice chest of food they'd brought for the festivities.

"You two must have cooked all night," he said, groaning as he lifted the ice chest off the small wagon Ramona and Eva had dragged behind them.

"We did make a lot of food," Ramona explained while Eva stayed quiet. "I have appetizers and finger sandwiches."

"Oh, who lost their fingers?" he teased, his glance dancing over Eva.

"You're too funny," she finally said, remembering how he'd reacted to Becky being asked to sing a solo for the upcoming school program. Clams could talk more than this man at times. So why was he so chirpy today?

Before he could react Becky came running. "Eva, you're here. Teresa said you are a *gut* friend to her."

Eva touched Becky's shoulder. "We are friends, *ja*. I met her when I first arrived."

"You met us, too," Becky said, smiling up at Tanner. "Even Daed likes you."

Tanner shrugged and shook his head. "She never misses a beat."

Eva took Becky's hands in hers and admired the girl's dark blue dress and black apron. "I did meet you then, and I'm so glad of that." She glanced at Tanner. "A lot has happened since that day."

"And you'll stay forever, right?" Becky said. "You're my favorite nanny."

Eva let out a gasp and glanced at Tanner. His expression was as blank as some of the boards he kept in his workshop. "I don't know how long I can stay, but I could be here longer than I'd planned. I might add a few weeks."

"Is that forever then?" Becky asked, glancing from her *daed* to Eva.

Tanner chuckled, his eyes on Eva. "Sometimes a few weeks can feel like forever and sometimes time goes by too fast."

Now Eva had to figure out which of those two categories referred to her. Maybe he was biding his time until she could leave. She leaned down and said to Becky, "I might have to go home since my *mamm* misses me, but now that I know the way here, I'll *kumm* back often enough."

Becky bobbed her head. "You could bring your *mamm* with you." Becky dug a toe into the grass. "Or she could get on the bus and *kumm* here soon. Then you wouldn't need to leave. You can't miss our school program. I'm singing, remember?"

Ramona let out chuckle. "Out of the mouths of babes." Then she gave both Eva and Tanner a knowing glance. "Becky, will you help me with the brownies I brought? Show me where the dessert table is located."

"Okay," Becky said. "Daed found that one right off."

Ramona let out another hoot of laughter as they hurried off together.

Tanner turned back to Eva. "You know, I was hasty in hiring you to stay with Becky."

Eva's heart did the let-down dance. He did want her gone. "Are you finally coming to your senses?"

"I'm not sure what's happening with my ability to think, but I didn't take into consideration that you'd have to leave one day."

"Neither did I," she replied. But in her mind, she thought about what it could feel like if she decided to stay. Would Mamm allow that? "But Tanner," she went on, "I've told Becky I might be here only through late spring, so she would know and remember that I can't stay. After that, I'll need to get back to help Mamm with our little vegetable garden. We always plant and store vegetables for winter."

"I'm glad you're addressing that with Becky. She takes to people better than I do."

"Really? I haven't noticed that at all."

He smiled after she let go of a grin. "You are both a pest and a pleasure to be around."

"I'll take that as a compliment," she said as they walked up to the big picnic table laden with all sorts of dishes, some covered in pretty wire domes to keep flies away. She was like a pesty fly to Tanner, she decided, buzzing around him and annoying him. And yet, he seemed to tolerate her.

His gaze held her. "It was intended as one, *ja*."

"Are you okay with her singing a solo?" Eva asked.

"I'm trying to be. I'm not one to be in the spotlight, so I worry about her. But she's more outgoing than me. I stuttered as a child and people made fun of me. Even now it happens when I get upset or nervous."

"But you've learned to control it," Eva said. "I've never noticed it."

"That's one of the reasons I don't talk a lot. A doctor helped me overcome it, but I always was a quiet child. I guess I learned to hold my thoughts in my head."

"You can talk to me about anything," she reminded him. "I understand some of what you've been through, and what Becky is going through."

"I believe you do at that."

He helped her set out the rest of their offerings and then nodded before he went back to the cluster of men surrounding Isaac. But Eva caught something in his gaze before his eyes went blank again. A longing.

The same longing she felt in her heart.

"Eva?"

She turned to see Teresa running toward her, a light mint dress looking starkly pretty underneath her bibbed black apron.

"Hello," Eva called. Although Teresa was three years younger than Eva, she was way more sophisticated than Eva.

Mamm would frown on that word. "Plain means plain, Eva," she would say when Eva would mention buying a bright color to make a dress. "But here, bright colors mixed with pastels and white or black aprons. And flip-flops. Always with the flip-flops. She'd already bought a sturdy creamy yellow pair and a nice light blue pair. They were odd but comfortable shoes.

Teresa grabbed her by the elbow. "What are you staring at?"

"Was I staring?" Eva glanced toward Tanner. "I was more thinking than staring, I reckon."

"Or daydreaming?" Teresa's dark brown eyes brightened. "Of a certain man?"

"*Neh*, no man. I'm not interested in any man. Trouble, that," Eva said, denial too strong in her words.

"And why not?" Teresa said with a sigh. "See that man over there with Ramona?"

Eva looked around. "You mean the one who's staring at us?"

Teresa giggled and waved. "He likes me," she whispered. "I met him at a frolic last week and he wants to visit me if my parents will allow that."

"You need to catch me up on this," Eva replied, intrigued. "He's handsome."

"He is at that," Teresa said. "And he has a *gut* job at the market."

"The big market?"

"*Ja.* He also has a nice little trailer house in a neighborhood not far from here. It's cute." Teresa shrugged. "I rode my bike by there when I knew he was at work."

"Sounds like you've found out a lot about him."

"I do my homework," Teresa retorted "I'm still trying to decide. His name is Jasper Porter."

"*Gut* that you got his name," Eva teased. "Why are you standing here with me and not over there talking to him?"

"I'm still debating," Teresa admitted. "I don't want to look too eager."

"*Ech, vell,*" Eva whispered. "Staring at him with those big brown eyes doesn't look eager at all."

They both giggled and started laying out food. When Eva looked up, she reminded herself to stop staring at Tanner. But it was hard to miss the man since he was a few inches taller than most.

Focus on Becky, she told herself. Not her father.

Still, her heart did that little dance that wanted her to be near Tanner. But not too near. She knew her feelings were new and raw and exciting. She wouldn't get carried away, since she couldn't stay here forever—even for a forever few weeks.

After they'd enjoyed fried chicken with potato salad and an array of side dishes, Isaac's children gathered around him while he admired the cake Teresa and her mother had made.

"*Denke* all for coming," Isaac said, his silvery beard twitching as he spoke. "I am a blessed man. My family is close, and I have many friends—some who live here and some who travel here. Now let's eat this cake."

And so they did.

Tanner and Becky got their slices with a scoop of vanilla ice cream on top and walked over to visit with Ramona and Eva. Teresa joined them after she'd served the cake.

"This is nice," Teresa said. "Eva, we can walk down to the creek if you want. It's really pretty."

"I want to go," Becky put in. "I like seeing the fishes and birds. Can I, Daed?"

"You don't invite yourself to places," he replied, his fears rising like running water. "Teresa asked Eva to go, not us."

"Us?" Becky giggled. "I said me."

"Oh, you did, didn't you?" He just invited himself, too. What was wrong with him these days? The more he tried to stay away from Eva, the more the world tossed them together. Well, this world was just a few blocks in the middle of a coastal city. Hard to avoid people.

"I don't mind," Teresa replied, eyeing Eva. "Do you, Eva?"

Eva gave Tanner a questioning stare. "*Neh*, not one bit. If Tanner agrees."

Tanner felt sweat popping out between his shoulder blades. "I guess you do need an escort. A big fish might jump up out of the creek and chase you all away."

"Daed!" Becky's giggles sounded like wind chimes. He loved seeing her laugh and smile. And she'd done more of that since Eva had arrived.

"What?" he asked, pretending innocence.

"The big fish live in the ocean," Becky explained. "And I can't go in that water anymore."

"Not until you learn to swim better," he replied, that memory making him want to hold tight to her. "But we can walk to the creek if you promise not to run ahead."

"I promise," Becky said, ice cream all around her mouth.

"Finish your cake and we'll get you cleaned up," Tanner replied, glancing at Eva. Then he looked at Ramona. "You might as well join us."

"Neh," Ramona replied. "I'll sit with my friends. But Teresa should ask that Jasper fellow to trot along since he's been following her like a puppy."

Teresa blushed. "I… I'd not thought of that."

"I'll send him over," Ramona said. "And I'll alert your *mamm,* so there will be no shock if she sees you with him. You'll be with others, so I'm sure it's quite proper."

"Denke," Teresa said, smiling. "Eva, your *aenti* is a kind, wise woman."

"Ja, she is," Eva said, smiling.

Tanner liked Ramona, but he could do without the matchmaking. "Becky, let's wash your sticky hands and that face."

"I can help with that," Eva said as if she had a duty to fulfill. "I'm glad you're going along with us," she told Becky. "You can point out all the amazing natural things to me."

Becky bobbed her head. "Teacher told us all about the earth and the skies and the big water."

"That's *gut.* You'll need to know and respect *Gott*'s world."

Tanner sat listening and thinking Eva was good at

pointing out the obvious. When was the last time he'd taken Becky on a nature walk? Back in Ohio, he'd lived outside just about year-round, what with chores and being an inquisitive youth.

His whole disposition had changed after Deborah died and Becky had been left as a baby without a mother. Thankful for his relatives stepping in, now he could see what he'd been missing.

Eva had given him gentle hints, and she was always kind and considerate to Becky.

Should he resent that? She was innocently trying to help his daughter, so *neh*, he couldn't resent that. But he could tag along with them and make it count. In more ways than one.

Chapter Fourteen

Eva tried to keep up with Becky, but the little girl was swift on her feet. They followed the walking trail near the gurgling creek, which looked more like a river, as it meandered through the woods toward the big bay.

Tanner talked to Jasper and Teresa but kept his eyes on his daughter. He hurried toward Eva but called out for Becky to slow down. Eva couldn't decide if he wanted to walk with her, or if he held back for propriety's sake. There could be talk, of course. But they were friends, and she did work for him.

Eva studied her surroundings, rather than the man who'd made his way into her life. This was a beautiful place, so peaceful and tropical. But her nerves jingled and purred, just being near Tanner. She had to get herself together. She'd had boys as friends, but Mamm always found something wrong with them and kept her at home. Telling herself she shouldn't fall for the first real man she'd ever been around, Eva decided being Tanner's friend was for the best. Just a friend and helper for Becky. She'd pour all her feelings into her work and Becky's care. Then she'd leave a piece of her heart here when she returned home.

Eva concentrated on her surroundings and waved to

several people on kayaks—little boats that reminded her
of canoes—but these were very colorful and not made
of wood. More of a hard plastic. She wasn't sure she'd
enjoy that kind of ride in such a wild place. The creek
beside them grew shadowy at times, thanks to the old
oaks covered with gray moss hovering over the water.
The area was both beautiful and mysterious, with moments of darkness and light.

Kind of like the man walking beside her, his gaze
on his little girl.

"Ospreys," Tanner pointed out as two hawks flew
through the trees and circled, searching for prey.

"Turtles," Becky said, running toward the bridge.
"They like to visit here in the sun." The child began
counting them. "Ten, Daed. I counted ten."

Eva laughed as she watched a huge turtle slide off an
old stump and disappear into the dark water near some
interesting trees. "What are those?"

Tanner glanced to where she pointed. "Mangroves.
They're all over Florida, especially in the Everglades."

Eva studied the strange trees mushrooming out with
tiny green buds, their roots jutting out of the water like
little hunched legs. "They looked all tangled to me."

"They are," Tanner explained. "Mosquitoes love
them and so do fish and snakes. They help protect the
coastlines when the big storms hit."

"And the Everglades?" she asked, wanting to learn
about this new world. "I've never heard of that place."

Tanner explained about the massive protected wet-
land farther down the state. "It's a brutal place, a
swampy place, but it's thousands of acres and holds a
lot of interesting creatures."

"The Everglades has big alligators," Becky added,
her arms stretched wide while she made a mean face.
"And they have the biggest teeth ever."

"I've never seen an alligator," Eva admitted, pretending to be scared. "We only have fish, turtles and frogs in Campton Creek. And snakes. I do not like snakes."

"We have those, too," Becky said with a shiver. "I don't want to see one."

Teresa chimed in. "But we do love the manatees. They are huge and grayish, like a big fish with a funny face, or a seal but cuter. But they usually don't show up until later in the spring."

"I have a lot to learn about my surroundings," Eva said. And she still had a lot to learn about Tanner Dawson.

"Let's see if we can find any butterflies." Tanner was probably trying to get his daughter off the scary creatures around here. "Remember how you love those, Becky?"

"I do," Becky said, giggling. "Daed calls me Butterfly, sometimes, ain't so?"

Eva laughed at that. "Well, you do flitter about, and you are as cute as a butterfly."

Tanner glanced at her while Becky held her head up, looking for any sign of her favorite insect. "I need to give you a nickname."

Surprised, Eva asked, "Oh, and what would that be?"

"I don't know. Little Bee, maybe. Or perhaps Blue Bird."

"I'm not sure I'm either of those things. I do like to stay busy though."

"Sparrow?" He stared over at her. "You're always interested but you fly away at times."

"Then you must be a hawk," she retorted. "Circling, but never finding what you really want."

"*Ach*, that hurt." He held his hand to his heart. "Do I seem that cruel and determined?"

"*Neh*, but you do seem distant and watchful at times. It's as if you're waiting for something to happen."

Tanner gave her an apologetic look. "Eva, I wish—"

"I see one. I see one," Becky said on a squeal. Then she was off to chase her butterfly.

And Tanner took off after her, leaving Eva to wonder what he'd been about to tell her.

"So what do you think so far?" Teresa asked, Jasper right behind her. He obviously had a huge crush. His brown-eyed gaze followed Teresa. It was sweet, really. Teresa deserved a nice fellow in her life and Jasper was cute, at that.

"I think this is a wild and mysterious place," Eva admitted. But her eyes were on the man in front of her.

"So mysterious." Then she smiled over at Teresa. "But… I like it here, all the same."

The next day, Eva helped Ramona with another tea, this time a group of Amish women who'd just come down from Shipshewana, Indiana. Five of them in colorful dresses and pretty crisp aprons, some wearing sneakers and some wearing sandals. They were so cute and prim as they listened to Ramona explain high tea. They tasted the delicious spread and sipped at their various flavors while she also explained the fresh herbs and how to make a great cup of tea.

"I could live with this," Eva said to herself as she finished cleaning the kitchen. She'd have to rush to get to the store before Becky was dropped off after school. After putting away the leftovers and checking that everything had been cleared, she freshened up and grabbed her canvas tote.

She was on her way out the door when Ramona called out, "Eva, your *mamm*'s on the phone."

Shocked, Eva spun around. She didn't have long to talk, but she took the cordless phone from Ramona.

"Mamm, is everything okay?"

"You didn't call yesterday," Mamm said. "I waited at the phone booth until it started raining. Got soaked getting home."

Eva let out a sigh. "I forgot. I'm so sorry. I can talk for a minute or two now."

"A minute or two? Where are you off to, and why are you too busy to call me?"

What to say? "I'm babysitting for a friend. A little girl named Becky. I'm trying to make my own money."

"You shouldn't be around children. They have all types of germs. I forbid it."

"Mamm, I've already committed to the job. I don't want to burden Ramona and she is feeding me and housing me while I'm here."

"You should just *kumm* home. This is silly. Do you think you'll get any better if you're dealing with a child all the time? I don't think so."

Eva took a breath. "Mamm, I'm not returning until the end of April, maybe early May, and I've already promised her *daed* I could help out."

"Her *daed*? Where's her *mamm* anyway?"

"She died a long time ago. He needs help."

"I don't like this one bit. You need to get home before you get too wild and independent. Put my sister back on the phone."

"I will, but I have to go. I'm late. I will call you at the regular time in two days, okay?"

"You'd better be back on a bus in two days."

Ramona took the phone with a knowing smile. "Now, Helen, your girl is doing great. She's healthy, no sniffles or coughs, and she's enjoying this nice warm weather."

Eva went on her way, her mind in turmoil. She wasn't

ready to leave Pinecraft yet. She'd made a commitment to Tanner and Becky. She ran toward the shop, her mind on getting there before Becky did.

But when she entered, Martha stood there talking to Tanner and Becky. They all turned to face her. Tanner had a solid frown on his face. She'd messed up yet again. And she was out of breath, at that.

Tanner dropped the frown and rushed toward Eva. "Are you all right?"

She bobbed her head. "Sorry. Phone call. My *mamm*."

"Martha, will you get Eva some water?" he called, his mind full of turmoil in the same way it had been when he'd watched Deborah die. "Now!"

Martha hurried away. Becky came running. "Are you sick, Eva? Did you get a boo-boo?"

"I ran," Eva said. "I didn't want to be late. I'm so sorry."

Becky tugged at Eva's skirt as Tanner eased her down on a chair by the dressing rooms. "Daed says don't run on the sidewalks."

"Well, I now know I'm not *gut* at it, that is for certain sure."

Tanner shook his head. "Don't scare us like that again. We were already concerned since you're never late."

"I'm just out of breath," she replied, acutely aware of the fear in his eyes. "I always manage to mess things up, so I didn't want to do that today."

"Is your *mamm* okay?" he asked, wishing she could see her value. Eva was one of the best workers he'd had besides his family members, but she seemed to live in fear of failing.

"I missed calling her yesterday, and now she knows I'm working for you and she's not happy."

"I see. So you haven't shared a lot with her?"

Eva glanced at Becky, then shot him a warning look. "I've talked to her about a lot, but she would not approve of me working all the time."

Becky stared up at her. "You won't quit, will you?"

"Neh," Eva said, "I want to sit with you and read to you, and we have our walks planned, and ice cream to eat, don't we?"

"We do," Becky said. "That will make you feel better."

"You are correct."

Martha brought the water and Tanner explained what had happened. Martha smiled. "I could use some ice cream."

Tanner groaned. "I guess I must make an ice cream run. I'll let them know it's an emergency."

Martha nodded. "We three will watch the store."

"Are you sure you three won't get into trouble?" he asked, concern still pinging in his heart.

"We'll behave, Daed," Becky said, grinning. "But don't let our ice cream melt."

"Neh, I will run fast, too."

"Neh." Becky put her hands on her hips. "No running on the sidewalks."

He did an eye roll but nodded before he gave Eva one last glance. "Don't overdo."

"I'm okay, really." She drank some more water. "I'll get busy straightening things. Becky can help."

Tanner smiled and watched as Eva and his daughter went off hand in hand, but he didn't miss the sadness surrounding Eva's eyes. What had her *mamm* really said to her?

Chapter Fifteen

"The strawberry ice cream was *gut*," Becky said later after they'd washed up. "Now I get to help fold?"

"That's the plan," Becky said. "We will start with beach towels. They are easy to fold if you know the routine."

Becky wrinkled her nose. "What's a routine?"

Eva wrinkled her nose back. "That means you learn over and over until we get it right."

"Like math and reading?"

"Exactly."

"Okay, then show me."

Eva checked the store. Martha was up front helping two women with sun hats. A couple of young Amish girls were thinking of buying some bathing suits to wear under their lightweight dresses, so they could go swimming.

She watched the girls while she showed Becky. "Take the big towel and fold it in two."

She gave Becky a smaller towel. "Your arms won't reach as far as mine."

Becky stretched her arms, but the towel was still too long. Eva motioned to the folding table. "Let's try this." She spread the colorful floral towel on the tabletop. "Now start at one corner like you are taking a sheet off the bed, but gently."

Becky picked up one corner. "Now what?"

"Bring it to the middle."

Becky did as she instructed.

"Now come around to the other side of the table and do the same with that side."

Becky primly walked around and lifted the corner and brought it to the middle. "It's still all messed up."

"We're halfway there." Eva tugged her side and brought it even with the bottom side of the towel. "Now you do that on your side."

Becky did so, and then ran her tiny hand over the terry cloth to make it smooth. Beaming, she said, "Almost done."

"See, all we have to do now is fold your side over my side, and then the pretty flowers will be showing. I'm going to count to three, and you bring your side over."

Becky counted with her. "One, two, three." Then she lifted her side of the towel and folded it over Eva's side. "I did it. I did it."

"Perfect," Eva said as she quickly straightened the folded material. "Now one more big fold and it is ready for display."

Becky squinted as she lifted the now-double material one more time. "It's folded."

"*Gut* job. Now go and place it on the beach towel table."

Becky slowly carried the pretty towel as if it were a crown on a cushion. Then she placed it on top of another similar one.

Martha came walking by with the two women. "That looks great."

One of the women stopped and smiled. "That's so

pretty, I'm going to buy it. I didn't notice those yellow hibiscus flowers when it wasn't folded neatly."

She beamed at Becky and Becky beamed right back. "I'm learning so I helped."

"You did an amazing job," the woman replied, her perfume smelling like the some of the flowers etched into the towel.

"Denke," Becky said. "We have much work to do."

"What a precious daughter you have," the woman told Eva.

She was about to correct the woman when she looked up to find Tanner standing near the cash register, his eyes on her.

But Becky took care of that. "This is Eva, my friend. My *mamm* went to heaven."

"Oh, I'm so sorry." The woman blushed and glanced at Martha. "I'm ready to ring up my items now."

Martha took over, chattering like a bird while Tanner turned and went through the swinging doors so fast, Eva could still hear the swish of him leaving.

Would he ever be able to let go of his pain and grief?

Tanner took out his frustrations on a huge arching driftwood branch he'd found after a storm had rolled through. He planned to shape it like a wave and place colorful handmade fish along the wood. He studied the weathered bark and as he always did, tried to imagine where this wood had come from. Maybe the yard of a home or broken from a huge aged tree on an island far away. How far had this piece of wood floated before it had finally washed up on shore?

He also wondered why driftwood had fascinated Deborah so much. She loved the gray pieces, her hand roving over each branch they found in the sand. Now he touched this piece, taking in the heat and the grain, his eyes closed as he thought of carving fish to place on the wood, his memories of watching his beautiful pregnant wife walk barefoot along the waves, her head down, her hand on her stomach.

Had she thought of him when she walked, or the other man, the man she'd really loved?

The door swung forward, and Eva came in. "May I speak with you?"

He wanted nothing more. "I'm busy."

"I can see that, but this is important."

He took his hands off the wood and turned to her, so many things crashing through his head. "What is it?"

"You heard what the *Englisch* woman said? And you heard Becky's answer?"

"I did."

"And it bothered you. Hurt you, maybe?"

Her eyes blazed with questions, but he wasn't ready to answer them. Lowering his head, he said, "I'm fine, just busy, as always."

Her gaze scanned the workshop then zoomed in on him. "You hide away in here."

Tanner picked up a tool and studied it. "I work here. This is my space."

"And you fill it completely."

That brought his head up again. "What are you trying to say, Eva?"

"I don't know," she replied in whisper. "I wish you'd talk to me. If we are to be friends, you need to know I am a *gut* listener. And I have plenty of room in my head and my heart to keep secrets. You seemed upset the other day when Becky mentioned singing the solo. That is a great thing—not something to be afraid of. Don't begrudge her of that because of your concerns. If you're worried, talk to me. No one else will ever know what you tell me."

Tanner swallowed, willing his anger and pain to go away. "Nothing much to tell. I loved a woman and… she died and left me a beautiful daughter who reminds me of her every day."

"Yet you cringe whenever your daughter mentions her *mamm* and heaven."

He had avoided that for a long time. "Do I?"

"I've noticed it. You got angry when she and I spoke of losing a parent, remember? I believe she wants to talk about her *mamm* with you. She needs to hear things about her *mamm*, from her father."

"Does your *mamm* talk about your father?"

If he'd meant to hurt Eva, he'd succeeded. She went pale, her eyes flaring and then fading out. "Only when I push, which I've learned not to do."

"You do seem pushy."

"I can be, when I feel the need."

"So why should I be any different? You of all people should understand."

"I do understand, but Becky is not me, and you still have time to help her with all that has to be going through her head. I never got that time or any answers, and it's part of the reason I came here. I needed to learn to be free of the grief and the guilt, Tanner. And so does Becky. The only way that can happen is to let her live her life and be a part of this community—in the singing and the youth frolics, and with all the people who love her. Especially you."

In his heart, Tanner knew Eva was right. But he did not want to deal with his heart right now. "Becky is my daughter. Just because you are helping out, doesn't mean you get to second-guess the way I deal with her or raise her, understand?"

Eva stepped back to give him an imploring look. "I know my place in her life. You need someone you can depend on, a stability for her. I will be that, for her and for you. But I don't agree with you on this issue. She's a little girl without a *mamm*, and she needs to know things. My *mamm* rarely opens up to me about anything, and when I ask she reminds me I am to honor her. But how can talking about a loved one who died be dishonorable—to that person or the people they have left behind? What is so wrong with wanting to know about the parent you never had an opportunity to be around? I wish someone could tell me why that is so hard?"

"You want someone to tell you," Tanner said, anger boiling deep inside his soul. "I loved her mother. I loved Deborah, even before we married. And I love Becky because she is a part of that. She is Deborah's daughter. But it hurts too much to talk about this. I don't want to upset Becky or confuse her. She knows her *mamm* is in heaven, with *Gott*, and she knows I'm here on earth with her. That is all she needs to know."

"You're wrong," Eva said, lifting her head, her gaze holding his. "I wish my *mamm* would talk to me, help me understand why I had to grow up without a father, why other children teased me or felt sorry for me, why she shielded me and held me back when I needed to grow and thrive. I know you want the best for Becky, but you can't see it from the same perspective as me, Tanner."

Tanner dropped the gouge chisel he'd picked up. "You're right on that. We have a different perspective. If you ever have a child, you'll understand a lot better."

Eva gasped and gave him another hurt look, causing him to flinch at what he'd just said.

"I might not be married with children, but I know what has hurt me all my life. I can see that same hurt in Becky if you don't change things. But I'm just here for a season to keep her company. I have overstepped."

She turned and left the room, the doors moving with such a rush, Tanner knew if the door hadn't been on a hinge, it would have been slammed in his face.

"You are a dolt," he said to himself. And yet, he couldn't bring himself to go after her and apologize. She was right about one thing. It hurt. Always it hurt.

But he couldn't tell her the difference between his protective nature and that of her mother.

He had to protect Becky's name and he had to keep her safe as his child.

Even if she did belong to another man. All the more reason, because of that secret, and because that man had died before he ever knew Deborah was carrying his child.

A few days later, Eva went to find Becky. She'd left her in the office behind the cash register since Martha was close by. Now she found Becky coloring pictures— flowers and birds and what looked like the sea behind them.

"Are you going to walk me home?" Becky asked. "Martha told me Daed is working on a big piece of wood today. He needs more time."

"I could do that," Eva said, wishing she could run away and not look back. Tanner would never approve of her, even though he'd hired her. The man must have been desperate. He could go back to letting his kinfolk help with Becky, if he felt Eva had asserted her opinions too much. But he just avoided everyone, all the time. "I'll check with Martha first. We don't want to upset your *daed*."

"He's always upset about something," Becky replied, her eyes wide with a bluntness Eva respected. And with a worry she knew all too well.

"I will find out what he expects," she said. "I'll send Martha to ask him."

"Because he's grumpy?"

"*Ja*, exactly."

Martha stuck her head in the room. "Did I hear my name?"

Becky bobbed her head, but Eva spoke up before the child told all. "I don't know if Tanner wants me to take Becky home or not. I haven't talked to him all day."

Martha took the hint. "I'll just go and check. Sometimes he does stay late. His family usually gets this one home and fed at those times. Let me see." She gave Eva a knowing nod.

At least someone knew what to expect from the man. She hadn't a clue, and that was frustrating. That and the way he made her feel, at times as if she was the only person in the world, at other times, as if she was the worst person in the world. Which way did he want things? That would be her next question to him. Did he want her here or not? And she'd get the truth this time, no matter how the man made her feel.

Chapter Sixteen

Tanner heard Martha's question about Eva walking Becky home, but he didn't know how to answer it. "I'm not sure."

Martha did a tsk-tsk and shook her head. "You hired her, Tanner. She's capable, sweet as honey and willing to help in any way. This woman is learning how to deal with life on her own terms, now that she has room to breathe and become herself. I've worked with her for a while now, and Eva is a *gut* person and worthy of your trust."

"Am I necessary in helping her, then?"

"You seem to be. You don't want to be around her, and yet, you managed to keep her nearby. What's up with you, Tanner?"

Tanner knew he must be confusing everyone with this push and pull he had with Eva. He wanted to push her away, but yet he couldn't send her away. His vow to never let another woman into his heart had gone weak, like the last flame of a candle burning out.

A grunt escaped before he could tamp down his aggravation. "Today, I'm trying to get this piece of wood shaped into a work of art. But so far, I have been interrupted over and over."

Martha looked aggravated herself. "Your daughter is tired and ready to go home. What should I tell Eva?"

Tanner threw up his hands in defeat. "She can take Becky home and wait for me there."

"See, that wasn't so hard now, was it?" Martha asked.

"*Neh*, I suppose it wasn't."

He watched Martha walk away, then stood and stared out the window. If he fired Eva now, it would only make things worse. Becky would be sad, and he'd be embarrassed and ashamed of himself. Deborah used to tell him he was too blunt and callous with his words. But words came hard for him. His family had been stoic and silent for the most part. So he'd learned to keep all his thoughts and feelings buried deep, because when he did speak he'd stutter, and his friends would tease him.

But he'd overcome that, thanks to his doctor and a teacher who helped him learn how to relax and form the words. Why couldn't he do that whenever Eva was around?

Talk about questions that needed answers. His family had not approved of his feelings for Deborah. Daed told him she was too wild and flirtatious, that she'd break his heart. And Daed had been correct. Deborah fell hard for someone else and left Tanner spinning in her fragrant dust.

Until the day she'd shown up on his doorstep here, asking for help. The kind of help that binds a man and a woman together forever.

He watched as Becky and Eva strolled toward his house. They were laughing and smiling. Becky lifted her finger and pointed out a hibiscus bush with an early vivid pink blossom. Eva touched the lone flower and smiled. Then Becky took Eva's hand, and they kept walking.

His daughter trusted Eva in a way Becky had never

trusted anyone else. She loved her family, but something about Eva's innocent nature had grabbed at his
daughter's heart.

And his heart, too, unfortunately.

He wanted to run after them and touch the hibiscus
blossoms with them, cut flowers for Becky to put in a
vase while Eva and he made supper. He wanted that
with such a deep longing the shreds of his heart burned
from the pain of it.

But he couldn't have that. His heart could burn even
more if he gave it away again. Maybe he was protecting
his heart more than he'd tried to protect his daughter.
He guarded both.

Tanner went back to work. But he didn't work on the
piece of driftwood in front of him. Instead, he found a
small cylinder cut from a cedar tree, the scent refreshing and clean.

He'd been waiting to find a way to use the round
piece of fresh wood, thinking he'd make a small tabletop
or a stool for Becky. But an image popped into his head.
He took twigs and wood cuttings and glued them together to form leaves. Next he found enough thin wood
to carve the blossoms of a huge flower to place in the
middle of the round piece of wood. Over the next hour
or so, he spent time carefully painting the pieces he'd
merged together until he had a bright pink flower with
a yellow center. A rugged construction put together by
a confused man, but it looked like a hibiscus, one that
Eva could touch anytime she wanted.

Once the paint had dried.

Eva got Becky settled with a snack and a book while
she roamed around and took in the charm of Tanner's
house. It was small, but cozy, sparse but clean, and it

had a lovely fenced backyard with beautiful palm trees and blooming bushes. A feeder and birdbath provided entertainment as colorful birds pecked away and then took a dip in the round stone pot filled with fresh water.

Becky had given her a tour of her small bedroom tucked in a corner with a lot of windows. The room held a girly flair, so she figured Tanner's female cousins had worked on that. It was clean and neat, but full of faceless dolls, books and a few wooden toys she imagined Tanner had carved.

Becky had held up a battered pink furry flamingo. "Flammy is my favorite. She sleeps with me every night. I got her at my *daed*'s shop."

Flammy could have used a good brushing and washing, something Eva planned to bring up at a later time.

After she'd tidied up the living area, Eva checked the clock. It was getting late, so she opened the small refrigerator and found some vegetables and a bag of frozen chicken tenders. Soon, she had a casserole together and in the oven, and sliced bread buttered and ready. She made fresh sweet tea and waited.

Thankfully, she'd told Ramona she might be sitting with Becky until Tanner got home. Ramona had managed to calm Mamm down on the phone. And she'd called the shop to give Eva a quick report. "I held her off for two more weeks, but she wants you home way before full summer, Eva."

Eva hadn't told Tanner that yet. But she expected to stay up until the last moment. Full summer would mean crops to tend to and canning to start. She had to be home by then, whether she kept working for Tanner or not. She didn't want to go against her mother's wishes, but she didn't want to leave Becky. Eva had decided she'd be honest with her mother and tell her she liked her job, she planned to stay here a while longer.

She wasn't ready to admit she didn't want to leave Tanner either. She had to get such thoughts out of her mind.

As if he'd heard her thoughts, the man himself showed up and walked in and glanced around the wide kitchen and living area of his home. His perpetual frown changed to a look of disbelief. "Did you clean?"

"I dusted and swept the floors," she said, wondering if that would make him angry. "I only tidied your room a bit, nothing more."

Tanner gave her a quizzical glance. "I didn't hire you to do all of this, Eva."

"I don't mind. I had to do something besides sit here."

He looked guilty after that remark. "I'm sorry I was so late getting home."

"No bother." Would he tell her to leave now? "I like to stay busy, is all. And why not clean and cook a *gut* meal?"

Instead, he said, "That explains the lemony scent. Nice."

Shocked, Eva only nodded. The man was always surprising.

"She is *gut* at keeping house," Becky said from the couch. "And she made supper, Daed."

"Oh, so that would be the other *wunderbar* smell, I suppose," Tanner said. "I am famished."

"Then you should wash up and eat," Eva said. "I've set the table and the casserole is cooling on the stove. You have fresh iced tea, too." Gathering her tote bag, she said, "I'll just go and leave you to your supper."

"Aren't you staying?" Becky's question held a squeak of hope and a sweet plea that hung over the room.

"*Ja*, aren't you staying?" Tanner's question held a trace of fear and a longing that filled the silence between them.

Eva glanced around, trying to find a reason to escape. "I didn't want to intrude."

"You won't be intruding," he said. "I… I was rude the other day, so please, stay and eat with us."

Eva gave him a long stare and then lifted her chin. "One day, you will need to explain to me exactly how you feel about this arrangement, Tanner. I'm never sure from day to day."

"One day," he replied low so his daughter wouldn't hear, "I'll tell you that. Whenever I figure it out myself."

Eva shook her head. "We are a confused pair—that is for certain sure."

"*Ja*, I agree. But let's eat and worry about that later."

Eva nibbled her food and listened to Tanner and Becky talking. Tanner seemed intent on asking his daughter pointed questions so he could avoid actually speaking to Eva.

"I saw a butterfly today," Becky said, spreading her hands. "He was huge."

"That big, *ja*?" Tanner asked, grinning.

He'd washed up and now his hair was still damp, but his eyes were bright with love for Becky. Eva wished he'd send her a kind glance now and then. She'd angered him in so many ways and he surely had not gotten over that yet. But he'd felt obligated to have her stay for dinner. Why? So he could torment her by being kind? Even after she'd chastised him. Even after he'd reminded her she was not a parent.

"Why aren't you eating?" Becky asked Eva. "Your casserole tastes great."

"I suppose I'm tired," Eva said, looking at her plate. "It's been a long day."

Tanner's smile fled and left a frown in its place. "Why didn't you say so?" He glanced out the window. "It's almost dark."

"I know," Eva said, standing with her plate. The sky had turned a rosy pink all mixed in with golden and blue hues. Another perfect sunset. "Ramona will be worried. I should go."

"We'll walk you home," Tanner said, standing to bring the dishes to the sink. "I'll clean up after we get you home."

"I can walk alone," Eva said. "It's not that far."

"But this is the city, Eva." Without saying another word, he looked outside and then back at her. "Becky, put your sneakers on. We're going for a walk."

Eva didn't argue with him in front of Becky, but once they were on their way up the street she waited until Becky ran ahead and then turned to Tanner. "Are you still angry after I got into your business the other day?"

He let out a sigh and then stared into her eyes. "I'll probably always be angry. But I shouldn't take it out on you."

"I was wrong to push you. It's none of my business and we've been at odds since the day we met. I still can't understand why you hired me."

"I hired you because I see the goodness in you, Eva. Becky sees that, too. And while I love my aunt and uncle and my cousins, I know they have busy lives, too. You came at the right time. Martha works in the shop and does what she can, and my other cousins work part-time at the market. So it's always a challenge to see who'll watch out for Becky. My aunt and uncle do what they can, but they are getting on in age. We'd already been discussing getting help when you showed up."

Eva was in awe of this man talking for so long and explaining things to her. "So, if you think I'm the person to help, why do we always seem to disagree?"

"I'm not at odds with you," he said, his voice low while Becky sang softly as she marched ahead. "I'm confused."

Eva knew it had taken a lot for him to admit that. "I'm confused, too."

Tanner looked ahead at Becky. "You and I are what one of my customers calls introverts. We like our quiet time and we're not big on frolics or get-togethers."

"I can agree with that." She kept an eye on Becky, too. "But I was never offered a lot of frolic time or get-togethers. Now I'm beginning to enjoy those things. And I like meeting the people who shop at your store. Well, most of them."

He laughed. "You probably know how to handle them better than I do. I like my workshop time."

"That's okay by me," she said. "I was only concerned for Becky's sake." Then she found more courage. "So, are you saying we don't get along because we're so alike? Or that you'd rather not be bothered while you're working? Or is it just me, Tanner? You don't want to be bothered by me?"

They'd reached the corner near Ramona's house. He turned to face her, the scent of roses nearby. "One day, Eva, I'll take you to the beach and explain everything. But for now, can you trust me? I'll try to do better by Becky if you'll try to understand that I like you, I want you to continue working while you are here. Having you for a few more weeks will give me time to find a permanent sitter for Becky." He stopped, took a long breath and said, "Remember, I have a lot on my heart."

"I will try to keep that in mind," she replied. "But Tanner, I won't be able to stay here much longer. My *mamm* is already wanting me to come home."

"So I need to be looking soon for someone to replace you."

She had thought he'd miss her, not just her help. "I suppose you should." She'd hoped he'd ask her to stay, even if they could never be together. Eva loved it here. She had work she enjoyed and taking care of Becky was a blessing. "I can stretch this out until May. I'd need to leave the last week of April."

Tanner had to think ahead and decide what was best for Becky. He'd forget all about Eva once he found another person to take over. He nodded, but didn't speak.

Becky turned to them. "We're here. Can we visit with Ramona?"

"Neh," Tanner said, back to his gruff self again. "It's way past your bedtime. Let's thank Eva and let her get inside."

"Denke," Becky said, hugging Eva.

"I enjoyed myself," Eva told her, her gaze moving over Tanner's stony face.

One step forward and two steps back.

"I will see you both tomorrow afternoon," she said, waving as she hurried up the steps.

When she turned at the door, she watched as Tanner and Becky walked hand in hand back home. How she longed to run after them and take Becky's other hand. Her heart ached with that need, that longing.

I have a lot of love to give.

But would anyone ever want to love her?

Did Tanner have any real feelings for her? Or as he'd

said, she'd been in the right place at the right time, and he'd been desperate enough to hire her?

Eva knew *Gott*'s will would provide, but she planned to put a lot of love into the time she had left here in Pinecraft with Tanner and Becky. A lot of the love she had in her heart, so she'd have the best memories when she had to leave.

Chapter Seventeen

Another week went by, and Eva had a routine going. So far, Ramona had stalled Mamm's commands about Eva coming home sooner. Eva calculated her time left here. If she stayed until May, she'd be here close to three months. But already she loved everything about Pinecraft.

The people were friendly, and the town buzzed with an energy all its own. The Amish blended with the Mennonites and the *Englisch* in a worldly way that she enjoyed. But she held to her standards and her faith. At least Mamm had taught her well in that respect. And…she did miss her mother at times. But she made it a point to talk to Helen at the required time at least twice a week. Mamm had become more animated and talkative lately. Maybe being alone with her quilts and other sewing had given her time to miss Eva—not just the fussing over Eva part.

Meantime, Eva had fallen into a rhythm that worked. Each morning, she helped Ramona with the baking and the preparation for the afternoon teas as needed. Then she rested for a while before walking to the Dawson Department Store. There she went to work on cleaning and straightening the racks and shelves, hanging items, rearranging displays and keeping busy until time for her to walk the short distance to the school to meet Becky. Yes, she'd been elevated to actually meeting Becky at the school gate.

They laughed and talked and sometimes stopped for ice cream. Eva tried to keep Becky outside as much as possible or in the little corner they'd created in the clutter of Tanner's office. He'd made Becky a small blue Adirondack chair and added a larger one for Eva. They could read or do homework there in the corner where Eva had set up a side table as a desk, complete with a small chair. Becky bragged that her teacher was pleased with how her reading had improved.

"I told Rachel you have helped me so much, Eva," Becky said with her arms reaching wide. "This much."

"That's a big much," Eva had said, after laughing. "But I'm glad we work well together."

Tanner stayed away from them for the most part. Every once in a while, he'd join them at the picnic table for ice cream or cookies. But he'd only sit and smile and listen to his talkative daughter. Sometimes, Eva would glance at him and find him gazing at her.

Contentment. That's what Eva felt, and she could see it more and more in Tanner's eyes, too. They'd agreed to disagree, but she knew she'd won his trust the day he told her she could pick up Becky at school.

Now if he would only trust her with his secrets. She had pieced things together enough to know that he and Deborah had married because of Becky. But they'd loved each other. Did he regret what they'd done? Did he regret that Deborah had died and left him to raise Becky alone? Loving her and losing her was grief enough but knowing they could have had a life together with a proper marriage and then children had to be eating at him, too. Maybe what Tanner needed the most was forgiveness. And he'd probably never really asked for that. Could that be his secret—that he'd never confessed and asked for true forgiveness? Or was it that he couldn't forgive himself?

She wanted to ask Tanner that, but he'd made it clear he didn't want to share anything much with her. Or anyone for that matter.

"What are you thinking over there?" Ramona asked now as she breezed into the kitchen all bright and cheery. She'd been busy in the pantry making a grocery list.

Eva looked up from her thoughts. Like a spoiled cat, she enjoyed resting in her favorite spot by the window. "Actually, I was thinking about how content I am. I've only had that light sniffle after the ocean, and I came close to a panic when those kids harassed me at the store. Then the one almost panic attack the day I was late to work. I'm breathing easier and I don't feel that weight of worry I always have back home."

She didn't mention that Tanner had calmed her down both times.

"You've learned to relax," Ramona said, nodding as she made a cup of cinnamon tea. "That's a *gut* thing."

"*Denke* for talking to Mamm," Eva said. "She tends to forget I'm in my twenties now and fully grown."

"You will always be her little girl," Ramona said. "But I think she's trying to let you go from her apron strings. And, Eva, she's been talking about someone else a lot each time she calls."

"Really? Who?"

"Moses."

"Moses, the neighbor she doesn't like at all?"

"The one and only. Seemed he fell and hurt his ankle,

so Helen has been feeding him and helping with his animals."

Eva burst out laughing. "You mean my *mamm*, who hates animals and wouldn't let me keep a stray dog, is helping her worst enemy with his goats?"

"And they're talking about making goat milk soap together. Moses thinks there's a market for it. Soap, lotion, all kinds of things. Your *mamm* has some ideas of her own." Ramona chuckled. "Scandalous, isn't it?"

Shocked, Eva sat still. "Why hasn't she mentioned any of this to me?"

"I think she's found an outlet for her need to hover, so she's afraid you'll judge her or think badly of her. She doesn't want it to look like it's more than it really is."

"Do you think it's more?" Eva asked, her head spinning.

"I do believe I hear a happy tone in her sharp words," Ramona admitted. "She's found someone else to save."

Eva's heart skipped a few beats. "That explains the happy tone I have heard in her voice, too. Then maybe she won't mind if I stay here longer."

"I don't know about that," Ramona replied. "But don't let her bully you to come home. She's not suffering overly much."

"Should I ask about Moses?"

"*Neh*, I promised I wouldn't repeat what she's told me. Mind now, she's only reported the facts, nothing else. And she duly complained to make it look like a big sacrifice. She's not ready to admit they might be friends after all."

"I won't say a word," Eva replied. "But I'll listen for hints next time I talk with her."

Ramona dipped her chin in a nod. "Now, let's get to baking, shall we?"

"*Ja*," Eva replied, her head full of all the ways she

could convince her mother that she was happy here. "Teresa is coming to help, remember? She needs the extra money."

"And I need the dependable help," Ramona replied. "Teresa has saved my bacon many times."

Eva didn't ask what that phrase meant, but she took it to mean Teresa was a great helper.

A knock on the side door to the kitchen showed Teresa's smiling face peeking between the sheers covering the paned door.

"Kumm," Eva called, smiling.

Teresa entered, in a good mood as usual. *"Gut daag."*

"Morning to you, too," Ramona said as she pulled things out of the propane refrigerator. "Now we have many tasks."

Ramona put Eva and Teresa to work on getting the tearoom ready for the next group of women while she finished baking the bite-sized pecan tassies they'd serve at the tea.

"A birthday party. One of them is turning sixty. They're all from Louisiana and they come down to Florida every spring. They love tearooms, so we're next on their list. Mind you, they are not the stoic, dignified types. These ladies like to have fun. I want them to keep coming back since they have money to burn."

"We'll make sure they like our service and our food," Eva promised. "They sound fascinating."

Teresa nodded, her dark eyes full of sparks. "I hope I can laugh and have a *gut* time when I'm sixty. That's so old."

"Watch it," Ramona teased. "I'm there myself."

"Okay, what's up with you?" Eva asked Teresa after Ramona had gone back into the kitchen.

"Jasper and I are officially walking out together," Teresa said with a dreamy smile. "He has explained that he makes *gut* money at the market and even does some handyman work on the side. His home is neat and clean—Mamm and I made sure of that when we took food the other day. It's not huge, but doable."

"You've got it all figured out then," Eva said, wishing she could look toward some kind of future that held promises.

She thought of Tanner and Becky. *Are they my future?*

Too soon? Or not soon enough? She'd keep praying on the matter.

Teresa went on, describing how Jasper had brought her candy and they'd walked on the beach, their *mamms* sitting on a bench nearby. "It's *wunderbar gut* to be in love, Eva."

Eva laughed, happy for her friend. "I'm so excited for you." It seemed a bit rushed, but Eva did believe in love at first sight. And why did Tanner's frowning face pop into her head?

"One day, you'll be the one telling me you're in love," her friend said, her smile all crunched up as she eyed Eva.

"I don't know."

Eva wished that with all her heart. But she needed answers before that could happen. And Tanner wasn't an answering man.

But was Tanner the man for her?

"Okay, the pecan tassies are cooling on the counter," Ramona said. "Let's set up the two round tables up front. We have eight women, so four to a table. The ladies like to chat back and forth. And be careful around their hats. They make new ones every year and the birthday girl gets to pick the winner of the best hat."

"What's the prize?" Teresa asked, her tone full of wonder.

"A freshly baked cheesecake which she has to share with everyone."

"Oh, and birthday cake, too?" Eva paced back and forth, carrying dishes.

"They have the birthday cake here. Then they take the cheesecake home to their condo for later. A great plan since it seems, from what they've told me, they like to stay up half the night, talking and laughing."

Eva bobbed her head. "I'd like some cheesecake later myself."

"I'll see what I can do," Ramona replied with a wink. "Now if you get the tables ready, we can take a quick break and I'll share a *tassie* or two with you."

"That can work." Teresa said with a grin.

A knock at the front door brought their heads up.

"It's way too early for the tea party," Ramona said, her voice echoing from where she'd bent to find something in the refrigerator.

Eva set down the butterfly-embossed plates they planned to use. "I'll go check."

She hurried to the screen door at the front of the long house and saw Tanner standing there shifting back and forth on his brogans.

"Tanner? What are you doing here so early?"

He held his hat in his hand, his eyes burning through Eva. "It's Becky. She's sick this morning and I have a delivery to make to one of the condos out on the island. I thought she'd be in school, but she's home. I have a neighbor watching her right now. But could you *kumm*? I've tried everyone else."

Eva nodded and motioned him in. "I need to let Ramona know. I'm helping her set up a tea."

"Then you can't come?"

Eva saw the apprehension in his eyes. She'd never

seen Tanner flustered, but when it came to Becky the man fell apart.

"I think we can make it work," she said. "Let's go back to the kitchen and I'll get you some fresh lemonade."

He followed, but probably didn't even register her offer.

"Tanner," Ramona said. "What a nice surprise."

Eva explained his problem. "Do you mind, Aenti?"

Ramona looked around. "The *tassies* were the hardest to get done. And you're almost finished setting the tables. Teresa, are you ready to learn the fine art of making finger sandwiches?"

"Ja," Teresa said. "But what if I mess up?"

"It's hard to mess up," Ramona said. "I will teach you. I can't depend on Eva for much longer, *gut* as she is in helping me, and you'll be a perfect replacement once she's gone. So let's get cracking."

Tanner paced with worry. He glanced from Ramona to Eva. "So you can help me?"

"Ja. Let me get my tote bag and a few sugar cookies for Becky. What's wrong with her anyway?"

"She has a cold and cough. Not sure how she picked it up, but she's miserable."

Ramona shot Eva a glance. "Be mindful of washing your hands and keeping Becky cleaned up. And make her some honey and lemon tea."

"I will," Eva replied, not sure how she'd handle taking care of a sick child. But she'd try her best. For Becky and especially for Tanner. The man looked like a walking pile of mush.

Soon they were on the cart and hurrying full throttle back to Tanner's house. *"Denke,"* he kept saying. "I have to rent a truck to get this big piece I made out to the condo. A heavy table. So time is ticking on the rental fees."

"You can drive a vehicle?"

He nodded. "I had to learn to do things differently down here. Sometimes, the buyer will pay for the rental, and I don't want to add too much on the time. I really appreciate your help."

Eva realized being a single man with a child could have its challenges. Tanner had managed up until now, but a baby Becky might have worked better with family members. A growing, energetic young girl would require a lot more effort.

"It's fine, Tanner. I'm sure Becky will be better soon. Just a cold. She loves being outside and the pollen is beginning to fall everywhere."

Eva had noticed that already. She hoped the yellow snow-like pollen wouldn't affect her own allergies and problems. But she had sneezed a bit yesterday. Why did she want to cough right now? *Neh*, Tanner would take that the wrong way. She cleared her throat and hoped she'd be okay. Becky needed her.

"She's never sick," he said. "Never like this. I think she has a fever."

"Do you have a thermometer?"

"I think so."

"I carry one with me."

"You'd know all about this, right?"

"Sure. But I'm not a doctor. She might need to visit one."

"We have a clinic here in town. Just up the street."

"I'll find out about it. Do I have your permission to take Becky there if she needs to go?"

Tanner gave her a startled glance. "Is it that bad?"

"I don't know yet, but Tanner, you need to calm down.

I want to have all the needed information. Children get sick all the time."

"Not my Becky."

"Tanner, slow down and listen to me."

He turned to stare at her. "What?"

"You can't be upset in front of Becky. You'll scare her. I'm sure she'll be fine. Why are you so worried?"

He glared at Eva and then his expression softened. "I'm sorry. I worry too much, ain't so?"

"Just a little, *ja*."

"It's just hard, trying to raise a child alone. I have a lot of people willing to help when they can. But lately, it seems she's growing up so fast and I can't keep up with her and the business, too."

"I'm here for now," Eva reminded him. "I'll take care of her. Ramona will know where to take her if I need to do so. I promise I'll do my best."

Tanner let out a breath as they reached his house. "I believe you, Eva. And I'm so glad you're here."

Eva nodded, her heart bumping too hard against her ribs. She was glad to be here, too, but she wouldn't always be around. Would he find a wife, just so he had someone to help with Becky? Or would he suffer because of what he considered to be his past sin? He couldn't save his daughter's *mamm*, and what if he couldn't save Becky?

Chapter Eighteen

Tanner hated to leave Becky. She was coughing and sneezing at every turn. Now she complained of a stomachache.

"She used to do that when she first started school," he whispered to Eva. "Something's up with her."

"She's sick, and she needs soup and sleep." Eva knew all the symptoms, but she'd need to sit with Becky and let the child tell her if there was something else going on. "Sometimes, coughing makes you feel as if you have a stomachache. I will read to her and calm her down."

Reluctantly, he showed Eva where he kept the pain pills and some herbal remedies Martha had insisted he'd need. "I have to go, or I'll miss meeting the condo owner on time."

Eva waved him away. "I'll go back in and check on her. I won't leave her side—I promise."

Relief washed through Tanner. Becky was in *gut* hands. He'd only be gone a couple of hours at the most. "Okay. I'm going."

Giving Eva one last glance, he saw the serenity and confidence in her pretty eyes. She must have had episodes like this a lot growing up. But she was brave after all. He wanted Becky to be brave, too. He'd have to curb his worries, or he'd ruin his only child.

"Denke," he told Eva again. "I won't forget this."

Eva only smiled and shooed him out of the house.

He hurried to his cart. He had just enough time to get the truck from the rental place up the road. But he couldn't help glancing back. Becky had been sick before, but usually his cousins just took her in and got her better.

Things were changing all the time. They'd all found steady work and his business continued to grow and thrive. He should be thankful.

How can I make my daughter grow and thrive? I need Your help, Lord. I need to trust in You. And I need to trust Eva with all of my heart.

He spoke this prayer as he went about his work.

Eva had become a part of their life for a reason. Tanner was beginning to see that reason. They needed her, and Eva needed them. It all made so much sense now.

Eva glanced through the partially open door to Becky's room. The child was asleep now. Her stomachache disappeared after some soup and crackers, and her cough and sniffles settled after some lukewarm tea with mint and honey. Wondering if Tanner had gone straight back to the store, Eva had read her the story of Noah's Ark, one of Becky's favorites.

"I'm so glad *Gott* saved the animals," Becky had said on a sleepy note. "I love the dove the best. It had a special job, ain't so?"

"That's right," Eva had replied. "It had to show Noah the flood had receded."

"So it brought the branch. An olive branch. Do olives grow on trees, Eva?"

"They sure do. The dove found a tree and plucked a branch, so Noah knew it was safe to leave the ark."

"I wish I could travel in an ark."

"The bus I rode in on was big like an ark."

"Maybe I can ride the bus with you one day."

Becky had drifted into her dreams, leaving Eva wondering about getting back on that bus. She'd have to return home, like Noah. Maybe *Gott* could give her a sign because she surely had no answers to her predicament.

She might be falling for this family—Tanner and Becky. They needed someone to love them. And she needed to be loved, to be a helpmate, to be a wife. Why had Mamm even suggested she'd never be able to marry and have children?

"I'll ask her that question next time we talk," Eva whispered as she went about cleaning. Then she decided she'd bake a cake and make a chicken potpie for dinner. Ramona had a really good recipe that she'd been wanting to try.

Tanner sent a message by James. "Tanner's having some trouble getting the piece set up. He hopes to be home soon. Martha and I have things under control at the shop."

Eva got busy in the kitchen, her mind on a nourishing supper for Tanner. She swept and cleaned until the whole house shone and smelled fresh and lemony. She even tidied up Tanner's room as quickly as she could without invading his privacy. But when she saw an Amish woman's clothing still hanging in the small armoire, Eva left the room in a hurry. She'd somehow missed that the first time she'd hurried through.

Tanner was having a hard time letting go of his grief. That made her want to stay busy, even more busy.

She found fresh strawberries and made biscuit-size shortcakes. A little fresh cream on top would be perfect.

She'd just finished when she heard Becky crying out.

Eva had checked on her not ten minutes before, but she hurried to find Becky flushed and warm. Too warm.

"Hold on, sweetie," she said. "Let's get your temperature."

Becky cried out again. "My throat."

Eva took a calming breath and touched Becky's forehead. "Hold this under your tongue."

Becky nodded, tears forming in her eyes.

To distract her, Eva started counting. Soon Becky was nodding with each count. When Eva thought she'd held the thermometer long enough, she tugged it out and looked at the gauge. One hundred and two.

She needed help.

After going into the kitchen where Tanner kept a business phone, she dialed Ramona's number. "Becky's fever has spiked. I think we need to get her to the clinic."

"I'll be right there," Ramona said. "I'll find a cart."

Tanner walked in the house later that afternoon, tired and frustrated. His day had gone from bad to worse when a traffic accident caused an hour-long wait time before he could get out to the island. Thankfully, no one was hurt badly.

Then he reached the high-rise condo and couldn't get the owner to answer the door. They'd agreed to meet at ten this morning. After borrowing the office phone, he'd located the woman who'd commissioned the massive table. She said she'd left to run some errands since he was late, so she'd be there in thirty minutes. An hour later, he'd still sat waiting on a bench by the truck he'd rented for two hours so he'd had to call the truck company and explain.

Now it was well past three. But he was home.

He noticed the food in the warm stove and noticed freshly cut strawberries in the refrigerator.

Deciding to check Becky's room, he found her bed empty. Panic set in. Where were they?

He went back to the kitchen and glanced around until he spotted the writing tablet propped up by the phone. *Tanner, we are at the clinic. Becky's fever got worse. I didn't have any way to get in touch. We'll be home soon.*

Eva had signed the note.

Tanner forgot how tired he was as he hurried out the door and practically ran the three blocks to the small clinic. He entered the jingling doors and checked the waiting room. No one. Then he ran to the counter and hit the bell. "Hello?"

A nurse came hurrying out of a room in the back.

"I'm Tanner Dawson. My daughter Becky is here with my friend Eva."

"Mr. Dawson, hello." The nurse motioned him around the counter. "I'm Margie. Eva and Becky are in the last room. Dr. Whitmore can fill you in."

Tanner hurried to the room and opened the door to find Eva, Becky and the doctor all looking up in surprise. "Becky?"

"Daed." His daughter's voice sounded strained and shrill.

"Is she all right?" he asked anyone who'd listen.

"She will be fine," the doctor said. "I've given Eva some sample tablets to use for the sore throat, and I've called in an antibiotic for the infection."

"Infection?"

Eva, who'd been sitting in a chair, stood up and nodded. "An ear infection that spread to her sinuses." She glanced at Becky. "I've had such when I was younger. They are not fun."

"Your little girl is sick," the doctor replied. "But treatable. Eva did the right thing bringing her here as quickly as possible once she spotted the fever."

"Fever?" Tanner couldn't believe he hadn't checked for that.

"She was fine one minute, Tanner," Eva said. "Then a few minutes later, she was too warm. Her temperature had gone high."

Tanner hugged Becky close. "I'm sorry I couldn't get home sooner." Then he glanced at Eva. She looked afraid. Did she think he'd be angry at her?

"Denke," he said, nodding toward her. "I knew I could count on you."

Her fear turned to a sweet blush of pink on her cheeks and a big flash of relief in her eyes. "I'm just sorry I didn't go ahead and bring her earlier."

"You did fine," the *Englisch* doctor said. "Fevers spike later in the day. But we've brought it down with the liquid pain reliever we gave her. Soon after Becky starts her antibiotic medicine she should start to feel better, but the medicine will need a few days to work." He looked at Tanner. "I'd like to see her back in two weeks. I'm concerned about that right ear."

Tanner didn't like hearing that. But he had to be strong for Becky. Eva had been right earlier. He couldn't fall apart in front of his child. He'd held up for so long, but he had to wonder if he'd shown any signs that Becky could have picked up on. He'd get a grip on that. Didn't he know he needed to trust—in *Gott*, and in the people who cared about him and Becky?

That included Eva now.

"Can I go home?" Becky asked the doctor.

Dr. Whitmore smiled and nodded. "I think home is the best place for you over the rest of this week. How's that?"

"Only if Eva will be with me," Becky countered without hesitation. "She can help me keep up with my schoolwork."

Eva glanced at Tanner. "I'm thinking your *daed* will make sure of that."

Tanner glanced at Eva with a nod. Then he lifted Becky off the examining table. "Let's get you home and we'll discuss all of this."

Becky bobbed her head.

Eva straightened her apron. "*Denke*, Dr. Whitmore."

"It was a pleasure to meet you and to take care of our Becky," the doctor replied. "Now, Becky, you can have a nibble of that strawberry shortcake you were telling me about. Just eat small bites so you don't aggravate your throat."

Seeing Tanner's questioning look, Eva said, "I told her what I'd made for dinner to keep her occupied."

"Ah, well, that sounds *wunderbar* to me," Tanner said with a grin. Relief and gratitude swelled inside his heart. He was thankful for Eva being with Becky all day.

But in his heart, he felt he should have been there, too.

"She's asleep."

Tanner came back into the small living area and watched as Eva made quick work of cleaning up their supper dishes. She looked right at home there in his kitchen.

He thought of other nights when Deborah had stood

there cooking, her gaze always off somewhere in the distance.

Eva glanced up at his words. "Poor little thing. She fought it, but the sickness won out." She stopped moving the dish cloth over the already clean counter. "Tanner, she'll be okay."

"I know," he said. "I was remembering her *mamm*. She stood right there when she was expecting. So beautiful, and so sad all at the same time."

Eva came over to him and took his hand. "You love her still."

Shocked, Tanner gripped her fingers and tugged her to the tan-and-blue-floral couch. "I will always love Deborah, but Eva, you need to understand something."

Eva's eyes went big and then he saw the resolve she managed to contain. "I'm listening."

"I loved Deborah, but she didn't love me."

Now it was Eva's turn to be shocked. "I see."

"It's hard to explain, but I want you to know the truth."

He studied her face, her eyes. Eva was so different from Deborah. More positive and daring, bold and determined. Deborah had only been determined to run away with the man she loved.

Eva stared back at him. "Are you comparing me to her?"

He had to smile. "I might be. But you are different."

"I know I'm different," she replied, her dander going up. "I haven't tried to hide that."

"I didn't mean it that way, Eva." He let go of her hand so he wouldn't do something stupid and tuck her into his arms. "You're so strong, even with your health problems. You came across the country for an adventure and here you are cooking and cleaning for Becky and me."

"I don't mind. I enjoy being busy. Mamm pampered me and rarely let me learn on my own. I learned a little when I insisted on it. But mostly, other women helped me along. I'd find excuses to visit friends just to go to the frolics. I saved money I made from selling desserts to neighbors so I could afford the bus ticket here."

"Your mother loves you too much, ain't so?"

"*Ja*. She means well. I shouldn't speak badly of her. I understand why she's tried to protect me so."

"Probably for the same reasons I try to protect Becky."

"I think so, *ja*."

"I love Becky too much, in the same way I loved her mother, but Deborah…she didn't love me. So I tried to overcompensate by spoiling her, thinking I could make her love me." He stood and looked out at the backyard where the fresh new buds were already popping out on some of the hibiscus bushes. "Spoiling isn't loving."

"Why didn't she love you, Tanner? You are a *gut* man with work you enjoy, productive work that brings joy to people, and the shop out front to sustain that work. I can't see anything wrong with you, other than that grumpy nature you use to shield your real feelings."

Tanner's heart swelled. Deborah had not complimented him much. She'd thanked him a lot for marrying her, but she had never actually cared about the rest. Gratitude was nice, but love should guide a marriage.

He shook his head. "You're right. I am a grump. It's the grief and my concerns for my child. I fear it might rub off on Becky. That or her mother's dour nature. Deborah was melancholy and sad a lot."

Eva's confused expression said it all. "Becky is like a little butterfly, just as you call her. She's always happy and flittering around. Nothing dour in that child."

"I'd like to keep her that way, but I can't spoil her to keep her happy. I need to be more involved with her. Firm and sure."

"You're a *gut daed*, Tanner."

He pivoted to stare at Eva, his heart lifting as he decided he had to trust someone. "Deborah loved another."

Eva stood, shaking her head. "You don't have to tell me this."

"*Ja*, I do. You've been so kind to us. Before I only allowed family to help, but Becky is growing so fast. I needed someone solid and sure. You are a blessing."

Her eyes widened and a soft smile formed on her lips. "No one has ever told me that before."

His heart hurt for her. She couldn't see her own worth. "Eva—"

"Tell me why she couldn't love you?"

He was about to confess when a knock came at the door. To the west, the sky streamed in streaks of golden orange flames. The sunset.

Tanner headed to the door. "Ramona, *kumm* in."

Ramona entered the room and glanced around. "I was concerned. How is Becky?"

"She's sleeping," Eva said. "I didn't realize the time."

Tanner nodded. "I'm sorry Eva had to stay here so long, Ramona." He explained what had happened. "It was one of those days."

Ramona chuckled, her gaze taking both of them in. "I can see that. Eva, you look tired."

Tanner studied Eva, realizing she did look pale. He should have gotten her home earlier.

"I'll be fine," she said. "Just sleepy."

"*Denke*," Tanner told her. "You should go with Ramona."

Eva nodded, her eyes holding the questions he still had to answer.

"Why don't you rest tomorrow," he said, his vulnerable feelings resurfacing. Why did he tell her all of this? "Martha and James can run the shop. I'd like to spend some time with Becky."

Eva gave him a confused glance. "*Neh*, I will work at the store as planned. Then you can have Becky to yourself." She looked hurt. Lowering her head, she turned to Ramona. "Let me get my bag."

"If you need us, let us know," Ramona added.

Tanner thanked them again and walked out onto the long porch, the sunset hovering in an afterglow as they walked away.

He stood and waited until they turned the corner, then he watched as the distant sun slipped like a lost beach ball behind the old oaks and swaying palm trees.

He was alone with his thought again and now he wished he hadn't shared so much with Eva. What must she be thinking right now?

Chapter Nineteen

She was thinking of all the reasons she needed to avoid Tanner Dawson. The man still had strong feelings for a woman who'd loved another. Confused about the whole thing, Eva got ready for bed. Whatever had been between Tanner and Deborah was a complicated thing. Eva had never loved that strongly, but she could see how it might happen to a person.

"Are you all right?" Ramona asked as she passed Eva's partially open door.

"I'm exhausted," Eva admitted. "I cooked and cleaned and tried to stay ahead of Becky's cold, which turned out to be more than a cold. I'll be fine tomorrow."

"*Ja*, because you will rest here all day until time to go to work at the shop. And if you aren't feeling up to that, you can go back to bed."

Eva nodded and yawned. "I'll be fine by morning."

After Ramona left, she curled up in her bed and thought about Tanner and Becky. Her prayers surrounded them.

They need help, Lord. They need someone to give them the kind of love that makes a family—a strong love, but a firm love, built on honesty and respect and

trust. How can I help? Should I help? I am confused
and afraid, but hopeful and determined. But Your will
has to be the final answer. Your will, Lord. Not mine.

She fell asleep with hope in her heart.

And she woke the next morning unable to breathe,
her throat raw with pain.

Tanner wasn't used to staying at home. He felt at
odds, but Becky was still asleep, and he didn't want
to wake her. She'd had a rough night, a scary night for
both of them. The doctor had warned she might find
some discomfort, so Tanner had rubbed her neck with
the salve the doctor had suggested. After he'd given
her more medicine, she'd finally drifted off to sleep.

But she'd asked for Eva.

"Eva had to go back to Ramona's house to get some
rest," he'd explained.

Becky didn't understand why Eva couldn't stay with
her. How did he explain the proper decorum, the rules,
to a child who only needed a mother? Eva would make
a fine mother one day because she'd been through so
much in her childhood. Losing her father, submitting
to her mother's misguided demands and being sickly
were more than one child needed to bear. But she'd overcome her fears to make this trip, to find her strength
and see how she'd survive without all the hovering of
a loved one.

Hovering and smothering.

He would not do that to Becky. If nothing else, Eva
had showed him that. And more.

Standing in the kitchen that felt so empty now, he
could still smell the freshness of Eva's cleaning. He'd
have to do better there. His bedroom was dusty and
dark, but he didn't want to stir up that dust now with
Becky so sick. Eva had straightened a few things, but

she'd respected him and left it alone for the most part. A telling gesture if nothing else.

A knock at the door brought his head around.

James stood there, shuffling on two feet.

"Aren't you supposed to be at the shop?"

James bobbed his head. "I'm not touching your workshop—I promise. I'm only cleaning up scraps, just like Martha told me."

Tanner was glad to hear that. He had a lot of dangerous tools lying around. "Okay, so where's the fire?"

"It's Eva. She can't work today. Ramona says she's sick and needs her rest."

"I figured that," Tanner replied. "She worked here tending Becky yesterday."

James pushed at his straw hat. "It's the breathing, Ramona said. I mean Eva's having some sort of breathing problems."

"What?" Tanner's mild concern turned to serious worry. "She's ill, too?"

"Very, according to Ramona. She wanted you to know."

Tanner thanked James for bringing the news. "Keep me posted and let them know I'm here to help."

He wanted to go and see Eva, but he couldn't leave Becky right now.

He could only stand here and wonder how Eva got sick.

Eva felt as if a truck had hit her. Her chest hurt with congestion. She couldn't find her next breath. Ramona had called a cab to get them to the clinic because Eva could barely walk.

The nightmare she'd fought all her life had returned to grip her. Mamm would want her home, but she wouldn't be able to get there in this shape. Nor would she be able to help with Becky or the store.

"We'll get you checked over and get some medicine to relieve you," Ramona told her. "I'll have to let Helen know, of course. You've already missed her call."

Eva could only nod. She hadn't felt this bad since last fall when the damp weather and a virus going around had brought on a flare of bronchitis. She wondered if she'd picked up Becky's sickness and why so quickly.

Dr. Whitmore came into the exam room and shook his head. "You're back so soon?"

"Ja," Ramona said. "And this time she's the one sick. Was Becky contagious?"

Dr. Whitmore tugged at his chin as he checked Eva's ears and throat. "Becky had a bacterial infection she probably got at school. A cold that turned worse, so yes, if you've been around her before yesterday, you could have picked it up unknowingly."

"I've been sitting with her for a few days now. And I work in her *daed*'s shop," Eva managed to croak out. "I must have picked it up quickly."

After Ramona told the doctor Eva's history, he nodded. "So you have certain allergies and something like a little bug can make that even worse. What about Becky's home? Anything there that you might be allergic to?"

Eva thought back over her day. "I cleaned the whole house, trying to get all the germs." She remembered doing a light sweep over Tanner's bedroom. "Dust," she said. "I did cough a lot in one of the bedrooms."

A blush ran up her cheeks as the doctor and Ramona stared at her. "It needed a *gut* airing. It wasn't dirty, but just dusty and dark. No light."

"Maybe a little dank?" Ramona asked. "Tanner is a widower," she explained to the doctor.

"Oh, that's right. Well, he might think he's going a good job cleaning, but dust can gather in a lot of dark places."

"I'll get on that," Ramona replied. "It's not healthy for anyone to be surrounded by dust, and here with the humidity, mold, too."

Eva felt bad for Tanner. He'd blame himself when it wasn't his fault. He'd probably frowned on any of his family cleaning his room, because he still had Deborah's clothes there in the armoire. The armoire Eva had opened out of curiosity.

If she told him the doctor's suspicious, Tanner would know she'd been in his room, snooping. Well, accidentally snooping when she'd been tidying the place. But she had mentioned going in there.

Right now, she was too sick to be embarrassed or worried, so she listened to Dr. Whitmore's advice and took the prescription he'd written.

She arrived back home with medicine and orders to take it easy over the next few days.

Despondent, Eva knew she'd have to return to Campton Creek once Mamm heard she was sick. Tanner would need to find someone else to take care of Becky, and sooner than they'd both planned.

She went back to bed and had fitful sleep the rest of the day. She'd had a brief time of being healthy and now this. How she hated this feeling of helplessness, of fighting for each breath. But the coughing and wheezing seemed to attack her from every corner.

Who would want a wife such as her? She'd be just as sick as any *kinder*, a double burden for any man. Especially a man who only wanted to protect his daughter because he still loved and needed to also protect the mother she'd lost.

* * *

"Daed, can we read the book about Noah's Ark again?"

Tanner glanced down at Becky with a tired smile. "I think you need to take a nap. Your medicine is working, but you need to rest a bit more. I'll read you a story tonight before bed, as I always do."

Becky looked sad but she nodded. "I wish Eva was here. She reads to me a lot."

"I wish she could be here, too," Tanner replied, meaning it.

Eva had become a big part of their lives in these few short weeks. He wanted to see how she was doing, but he also didn't want to upset Becky. So he waited and watched and made sure Becky was improving.

"Can we sit on the porch?" Becky asked, clearly getting her energy back.

"Not yet. You need to eat some soup and then take your nap. You can come into the kitchen with me while I heat up the soup Martha sent over to us."

"Chicken noodle. Martha says that will cure anything."

"Martha knows her soups—that's for certain sure."

Soon he had Becky giggling while they slurped noodles without using their table manners. Spending this forced time with Becky made Tanner see that as much as he loved his daughter, there was a trace of himself that he'd held back.

She would always be his daughter.

But she had belonged to another for a brief time. A man who never even knew he was going to be a father. Deborah never got the chance to tell him so.

And Tanner would always wonder what would have happened if the man hadn't been killed. Would he have run away with Deborah as she'd planned? Or would Deborah have still wound up at Tanner's door, seeking help?

It was too much. Too complicated. Too risky.

No one could ever know the truth. For Becky's sake. And maybe because Tanner had some pride left, too. He needed to ponder that and work it out.

A knock at the door brought him out of his musings. Ramona stood there with more food.

Glad to see her, Tanner invited her in. "I've scoured the whole place, so you should be safe." Then he lowered his voice, "I heard Eva is ill, too. How is she?"

Becky lifted her head. "Did I get Eva sick?" Then tears formed in her eyes. "That's why she's not here. I got her sick."

Ramona glanced at Tanner, and he let out a long huff of a sigh. Becky's tears fell down her face like a tiny waterfall.

Ramona put down the cookies and sandwiches she'd brought and rushed to Becky. "It's okay. Eva is doing just fine. The same nasty bug that caught you also got to her. But she has medicine, same as you. And she is resting, same as you."

"Why can't we be sick together?" Becky said on a wail. "We could read and take naps. I want her to come and see me."

"She can't," Tanner said with a sharpness he hadn't intended. "Eva needs her rest. Alone. And so do you."

Becky cried and tugged at Ramona. "Will you take her the book about Noah's Ark so she can read it? She loves the dove."

Tanner's heart fell apart at those words. He swallowed and took Becky into his arms. "I'll send her the book if you try to take a nap. Then when you are both better, we'll take a day to go to the beach. And stay far from the big waves, so no one will be sick again. Okay?"

Becky nodded. "Okay."

Tanner put her in her bed, got the book she wanted Eva to have, wiped it down and then came back out to find Ramona tidying the kitchen.

"You don't need to do that," he said.

Ramona turned and gave him a solid glance. "I do need to do this, and Tanner, you need a housekeeper. The doctor thinks dust and mold might have caused Eva's sickness. We can't be sure where Becky or Eva picked this up but starting at home is always for the best when dealing with germs. But if Eva gets sick again, she might not be able to do her job after all. In fact, her *mamm* will probably want her to come home right away once she hears this."

Chapter Twenty

Tanner didn't know what to say. "I clean house."

"I'm sure you do," Ramona replied. "But you're busy and your helpers can only cook and clean when they're here. I know it's been difficult lately. Eva is willing to help, but she is delicate. If you allow it, I can bring in a crew of willing women to get this place spic-and-span. No judgment, just friends wanting to help."

Tanner wanted to say he and Becky didn't need help, but if he'd learned anything over the last few weeks, it was that pride could bring a man to his knees. He'd shuttered himself here with Becky and he'd made do with very little cooking and cleaning. Ramona was right. His family had cleaned once a week and now that his nieces and cousins had moved on, he'd neglected things. Maybe he was the spoiled one.

"Tanner?"

He glanced at Ramona, swallowed his pride and nodded. "I'd appreciate that. It's time, I reckon."

Ramona had the good grace not to bob her head in agreement. "I'll get the ladies together. Maybe in a couple of days, after Becky and Eva are both better?"

"That would work." He thanked Ramona for the

food. As she was leaving, he called out, "Oh, wait. I have something for Eva. I made it a while back and I was saving it…for a special time. But maybe it will cheer her up."

He went to the back porch where he'd hidden the hibiscus carving and brought it back. "She seems to favor the hibiscus flowers."

Ramona took the piece of oval wood and eyed it. "Tanner, this is lovely. Eva will be so touched."

"Let me wrap it. Just brown paper, but I like to wrap the things I create to keep them safe."

Ramona smiled and helped him get the paper folded over the carving. "You have such a talent."

"It's a living."

"You have a *gut* living and, Tanner, you have a *gut* life. Remember your blessings."

Tanner thought about that. He did need to remember how blessed he was. "Tell Eva hello and I hope she's better soon." He hesitated, then added, "I promised Becky when she's feeling better, we'd go for a picnic near the shore. Maybe Eva will feel up to that, too."

Ramona studied him for a moment. "Do you have feelings for Eva?"

Tanner felt sweat popping out on his backbone. Not one to blurt out such private things, he stood still and stared out at the palm fronds lifting in the wind.

"Tanner?"

He turned back to Ramona. "I think I might, but I can't be sure. I've been on my own for a long time and well, Eva might rather go home to her *mamm*."

"Is that your excuse?"

Surprised, he gawked at Ramona. "She does have to leave, right?"

"She can make her own decisions on that, I'm think-

ing, but *ja*, Helen expects her back before full summer."
Ramona shifted on her tennis shoes. "But then, you've
known that all along. I know you care, but you can't
toy with her emotions. She's grown but she hasn't experienced a lot of life, understand?"

"I do and I respect that," he said. "She wanted work
and I needed someone to guide Becky. And not just
anyone. Eva has helped her with her reading and taught
her a lot of the things I've neglected."

"I'm glad to hear that," Ramona replied. "Just don't
hurt her. She's strong underneath her frail appearance,
but she's quite fragile in the love department."

Tanner understood more than he could say. "I don't
know if I can love that strongly ever again."

"Then you need to tell Eva the truth. All of the truth."

Shocked again, he asked, "What are you saying?"

"It's pretty obvious you're trying to protect your
child. But Tanner, you should know Becky is accepted
here. No matter what happened before she was born,
she is loved, and she will be protected here. Eva would
do the same for her, too."

Tanner lowered his head. "So you're saying I've held
a secret that everyone's already figured out."

Ramona shook her head. "No one is talking about
you if that's what you think. You and Deborah aren't
the first to get the cart before the horse. And Becky is
a sweet child. You're doing your best."

He didn't elaborate. So no one had questioned the
hurried wedding. They thought Becky was his child.

Tanner let Ramona go with that assumption. "You've
given me a lot to consider. I know you're doing this out
of love for Eva. I appreciate that. I can only tell you
I'm confused, but I do care about her. A lot. It's a new
feeling for me."

"New feelings can bring about new hope and the life *Gott* means you to have." Ramona held the package he'd wrapped and then said, "Why don't you wait and give this to Eva in person. Maybe on that picnic you're planning."

"That's a thought." He took the package back. "I would like to see her reaction."

Ramona gave him a reassuring smile before she left. He went to check on Becky. She was sleeping, so Tanner decided he'd go into his room and begin the process of cleaning. Not enough to stir up dust. But just enough to face his memories, and maybe let go of some of them.

"I'm much better."

Eva smiled at Teresa, glad to see her friend after four days of being confined to Ramona's house. "I've missed our walks. How is Jasper?"

"He is great," Teresa said, her dark hair in a perfect center part underneath her organdy *kapp*. She wore a navy dress and a crisp white apron with white flip-flops. "We've been seeing each other more and more, but we're taking it slow."

"I guess slow is *gut*," Eva said, wondering how Tanner was doing. "I miss work, too. I'm going back on Monday."

"So you have the weekend to make sure you're well."

"*Ja*, but I'm feeling so much better. And Becky is completely well."

"Does your *mamm* know?" Teresa asked, her eyes wide with curiosity and concern as she grabbed one of the lemon bars Ramona had left on the counter for them.

"I told her I got sick," Eva replied before sipping on her honey-infused tea. "She is not happy, but I've explained that I'm okay and I had enough money to pay my doctor bills."

"I reckon she wants you home."

"She does, but she took it much better than I expected. I think she's found someone else to lavish with love—the widowed neighbor next door."

"The man she always complains about?" Teresa let out a snort. "Your *mamm* sounds like an interesting woman."

"She is at that. But I must go home and check on her at least. If I decide to stay here, I'd move back after explaining things to her."

"And would you explain about Tanner and Becky—that *you* now have someone to lavish *your* love on?"

Eva put a hand to her lips. "Shh. People will believe that."

"Do you believe that?" Teresa asked. "I think you fell for Tanner the first day you saw him."

"I did not. He was rude."

"And yet?"

"And yet, I love Becky and *ja*, I care for Tanner. He needs someone to love him."

"And you would love him out of duty, or truly love him?"

"I'm trying to decide that," Eva admitted. "I think I love him, and it would be because I want to be with him—not out of duty or pity. He does not want pity or an arranged marriage. And neither do I. I know how I feel, but he's not ready to hear that—from any woman." She shrugged. "He is still pining for Deborah."

She couldn't tell Teresa all that Tanner had told her. He surely regretted being so honest with her. He'd pull away again. She knew his patterns and his moods now.

Knew his pride, too. He wore pride and guilt like a shield.

Teresa cleared their dishes and quickly washed them and put them on the dish drainer. "I think he will pine for you if you leave. You two need to sit down and talk about your feelings."

"I don't believe Tanner is ready for that talk."

"Well, if he doesn't hear it from you, you might go home and be lonely. Do you want that?"

"What I want right now is another lemon bar," Eva replied.

Teresa said, "Uh-huh. I think I have my answer."

Eva didn't deny anything. She couldn't even tell her best friend what she wanted these days. She'd had a lot of time to think about it and pray about what might come next.

Her here with Tanner and Becky.

Or her back home with Mamm and Moses.

She sure knew in her heart which she wanted.

But Tanner didn't want the same things she did.

The next week held perfect weather, so Tanner planned an afternoon off to go to the beach as he'd promised. After her follow-up checkup, Becky was completely well and back at school. They'd go to the shore as soon as she got home. Eva had worked a couple of hours each day, and she'd kept Becky with her in the shop. They were both being cautious. Eva and Martha cleaned down all the doors, the bathrooms and even the cash register. No germs could live in that store that now smelled like lemon and lavender.

Tanner had only spoken a hello and "Glad you're

feeling better" to Eva. He needed some time and so did she.

But now, he was ready to have a few hours away from the world and he wanted Eva and Becky there with him.

Tanner heard the chatter of female voices on his porch, so he hurried to open the door. Another reason for him and Becky to leave for a few hours.

"We have arrived," Ramona said with a beaming smile. "I have Rachel and your cousins Reba, Leah and Trudie. Martha will be here later after she closes down the store. Your home will be pristine by the time we finish."

"And I have arranged to go on a picnic with Becky and Eva," Tanner replied, searching the women crowded on his porch. "We'll be out of the way for a few hours."

"She's on her way," Ramona said. "She's packing a huge basket with your early supper."

"That's thoughtful," he said. "I just have chips and crackers."

"Then you will appreciate her efforts," Ramona replied as the women filed in. "She's much better and has energy to spare, so she'd cooked up a storm."

"Is she truly well?" he asked, still concerned for Eva's health. Still feeling the traces of his past life. "I haven't pestered her about it."

"She's fine. But her mother is wanting her home. So be prepared that she might leave soon."

"I'll have to explain that to Becky."

He wished he hadn't gotten so close to Eva, because now Becky expected her in their life. How could he explain yet another heartache to his daughter? Should he tell Eva the truth and let her decide what she wanted? Would she want him after he confessed his secret?

So many questions, and so much complicated confusion. He wouldn't blame Eva if she ran to the bus stop and left.

But he hoped she wouldn't. Not yet.

Chapter Twenty-One

Eva laughed as Tanner loaded the cart with the basket of food she'd prepared and their blankets and towels. Becky got in the back and grinned up at them.

"I'm so much better. Now I get to go to the beach."

"Same here," Eva replied. "You and I will stay well from now on, ain't so."

"I hope so," Tanner said. "I've never prepared so much soup in my life."

"It worked," Becky said. "Martha makes chunky soup. It sticks to your ribs."

Tanner rolled his eyes. "Martha also teaches my daughter all the old sayings."

"They do hold true," Eva replied, glad to see him in such a light mood.

She'd avoided him the few days she'd worked this week. He'd only allowed her two hours each day, and she'd stayed busy so she wouldn't think about him. Martha made her rest every hour and drink fresh orange juice and water. Becky had walked from school with two older girls, and she too, had to stay close to the shop. They had taken a quick break each day to get some sunshine and fresh air. That schedule had been doable since Tanner stayed in his workshop.

Now they were alone and headed to the beach, a place where Eva had been taken by the waves. And carried out of the water in Tanner's strong arms. So different from working nearby him.

"Are you really feeling okay?" Tanner asked as he pulled the cart up to the bus that would take them to the island. "I worried about both of you."

"I am fine now. It's great to be doing something just for fun."

"Well, the weather is surely cooperating. Look at that sky. No clouds and less humidity. It's a nice day."

Eva took a deep breath, glad it didn't bring up her lingering cough.

She got out of the cart and gathered the towels while he grabbed the basket and fussed with rearranging it before he took it off the seat next to where Becky had sat.

Once they had everything, he glanced at her. "You do look more rosy-cheeked."

Eva grinned, glad she'd washed her hair and worn the mint-green dress Ramona had made for her. "I'm taking my medicine and vitamins, and you know Ramona is filling me up with the best food and herbs, and her natural healing products. She insists I sit in the sun for at least ten minutes every day."

"Ramona loves you. I think she'll hate to see you leave."

Becky's head came up as they walked to the bus. "When do you have to go, Eva?"

Eva dreaded thinking about it. "I have about a month left if I stretch it a few days. I have to help Mamm with the garden. That's where most of our food for the winter comes from."

Becky's face twisted. "Is a month a long time away even if you stretch it?"

"I should be able to see your solo," Eva said, deciding she wouldn't miss that for the world.

"So it's coming soon—my singing and then you'll leave?"

Eva lifted Becky's chin. "I'm afraid so. I'm sorry."

"It's about thirty days," Tanner said, his gaze on Eva as he motioned Becky up the steps and into the bus. "Don't worry. I'll find someone nice to sit with you once Eva is gone."

Eva thought he was taking it in stride. Maybe to keep Becky calm. Or maybe he was ready to be done with Eva. She'd been more trouble than help, no matter how much he appreciated her.

"I don't want someone else," Becky said, her lips working toward a pout. "I want Eva to be my *mamm*."

Tanner and Eva both fell into their bus seats in silence and looked straight ahead.

Tanner took Becky on his lap as the bus started off.

Eva didn't dare glance at him, but Becky's blunt statement had her thinking of cooking in their kitchen every night, of tucking Becky into bed and then sitting in the swing with Tanner by her side while they enjoyed the sound of the palm trees rustling in the ocean breeze.

"I do," Becky said, emphasizing her words before they could form their own. She gave Eva a pleading stare. "I want you to be my *mamm*. If you were my *mamm*, you wouldn't have to leave. And Daed and I wouldn't have to be alone. We are a *gut* family, Eva. And I'll try to do better if you stay. I can learn to help more. Daed says I'm a *gut* helper."

Tanner shot Eva a glance that felled her heart. His eyes held a desperate silent plea all twisted up in his guilt and grief. He swallowed and looked out the window, his hand resting on Becky's head.

"You are the best helper," Eva replied. "I know that for certain sure. You are sweet to want to do your best. I love my time with you each day. Never forget that." She swallowed and tried to explain. "But being your *mamm* is a bit different than seeing you a few hours each day during the week."

"Is that why you're leaving us?" Becky scratched at her nose. "'Cause you don't want to be a *mamm*, ever?"

Tanner nudged his daughter's arm. "Becky, not so many questions. I've explained Eva is just visiting and I knew her job would be only for a while. Her own mother misses her."

Becky blinked back tears, her lip jutting again. "I wish she could stay, is all."

Eva touched Becky's face and tried to give her a positive smile. "If I do leave, I promise I'll *kumm* back to see you. You must remember that, okay?"

Becky nodded and turned her head toward her father's strong shoulder, where she buried her face. Tanner glanced over at Eva, but she couldn't read his expression. Did it hold regret or fear, or maybe both? What was the man thinking? Did he want her to stay, or was he ready for her to go home? She wished he'd just talk to her, let her know his feelings, let her into his life in a way that showed he cared. The man could switch his feelings as fast as a dolphin could flip through the water.

But then, she'd hidden her own feelings deep inside her heart. She'd never been in love before, but she knew one thing—loving someone could break your heart so easily. So quickly. So completely.

She wasn't sure she was ready for that kind of hurt.

And she wasn't sure if Tanner could go through that kind of hurt again. Eva took a deep breath and calmed herself. She'd enjoy this special day and let the Lord handle the rest.

Her faith was the only thing guiding her right now.

Tanner took another bite of his roast beef sandwich. The beef was tender and thinly sliced and loaded with pickles and tomatoes and some fresh cheddar from the market. The bread was homemade sourdough. Eva sure could put together a picnic.

He thought of Becky's very blunt, but earnest request. He could picture Eva in their home, in the kitchen each night. They'd all have supper together then maybe take a walk around the block or up to the creek. Becky could ride her bike, and he'd hold Eva's hand.

But Eva had whispered to him, while Becky walked ahead after they exited the bus. "She's young and impressionable. She needs a *mamm*, but I don't know if I'm that person."

Tanner could only nod. Eva didn't want to be married or saddled with him and a child. He couldn't blame her, but he wished she did want them. Wait? Did he want that?

"It is a big step," he'd managed to get out. Had he become tongue-tied and stuttering again?

"Daed, you're making noises with your mouth," Becky said, in a better mood now that she had a bucket and shovel to dig through the sand.

Tanner stopped smacking and stopped daydreaming. "Was I? I guess I'm really enjoying this sandwich. Might be the best sandwich I've ever had in my life."

Becky giggled at that. "You love all the sandwiches. He eats them with potato chips."

Eva smiled and dug through her bag. "I happen to have a fresh bag of chips right here."

Tanner tried to grab the bag. "Were you holding out on me?"

Eva held it back. "You may have some chips, but not the whole bag. I like them with my sandwich, too."

"We are supposed to share," Becky said, her hands on her hips. "And then you promised you'd take me into the water, so I won't fall down again."

"Okay, all right," Tanner said. "I give. I'll only eat a third of the bag, and that leaves a third for each of you. But I plan to eat at least five of those coconut-choco-late-chip cookies Ava said she brought."

"Then I get more than one," Becky replied, grinning.

Tanner stood and growled like a sea monster, causing Becky to take off running.

Soon they were all playing on the beach and trying to form a sandcastle with dirt and water. Tanner showed Becky how to make a shape with her bucket. Then they put shells and sticks on top.

"It looks like a cake," Becky decided. "A sand cake."

"We won't be able to eat that," Eva said, laughing as she sank down on a towel.

"Do you want to go in the water?" Tanner asked Eva. "I'll make sure you're safe."

Eva looked into his eyes with such an earnest inten-sity, Tanner knew he'd never forget her or get over her either. "I believe you will do just that," she said. "Even if it means watching me get on a bus to go home."

"What are you saying, Eva?" he asked, wanting to hold her here with him and kiss her. Which was ridic-ulous. Or was it?

The more he thought about it, the more he wanted that—to hold Eva, to protect her, to kiss her. To love her.

He'd gone and done the one thing he hadn't planned on doing ever again. He'd fallen in love. With Eva Miller.

Eva knew the moment she'd spoken, she'd made a mistake. Tanner's whole demeanor changed. He got up and called to Becky. Then he took his daughter to the water's edge and held her hand while Eva sat watching.

He'd obviously changed his mind about keeping her safe, but she was a grown woman, and she wouldn't venture out into the waves too far. So she stood and adjusted the old dress she'd worn, tossed off her flip-flops and walked to the water. While Tanner was busy with Becky, Eva stood at the edge and let the cool waves hit her bare feet.

She giggled at the feeling, the rush of water and sand washing her feet, cleaning her skin, making her smile. Closing her eyes, she let the sun hit her face as she dreamed of seeing this ocean every day.

"Eva?"

She opened her eyes to find Tanner standing there. Becky was sitting up on a towel in the sand. Not sure what to say, she looked from where Becky sat counting seashells back to Tanner.

His eyes held that mixed message of longing caught up in regret and grief. She had to accept that this man would never love again. She had to accept that she had fallen in love with him.

"What?" she asked so softly he leaned in.

"I don't know," he said, his palms up. "I don't know what to do about you."

"Then I'll make the decision for you," she replied, her heart hammering a song of regret. "Mamm wants me home sooner than later. I won't draw this out any longer, Tanner. It's not fair to Becky. I think Teresa would be available to sit with her. She and Jasper won't be getting married for a while and even if they do, Jasper's home is the next block over from yours. She can easily meet Becky at school and take care of her in the summer. She needs the work."

"I see," he said. "You've certainly thought this through."

"Well, we knew this day would come, didn't we?"

"*Ja*, we did." He glanced back toward Becky. "Just give us a little more time. I'll need to let Becky be around Teresa so they can grow close." Then he looked out over the waves. "And she does have her solo at the scholars' end-of-year program."

"I'll stay for her program," Eva said, nodding. "I don't want to miss that. She's practiced so hard. Becky is gifted with a lovely voice."

She turned to go back to the towels, but Tanner grabbed her hand. "I wish—"

"I know," she replied. "I know, Tanner. But wishes can't always come true, can they?"

Giving him one last look, she hurried to the table and started gathering their food into the picnic basket. She saw another bag holding a wrapped package sitting on the table next to the insulated casserole dish cover Ramona had loaned her. Eva stared at the brown paper inside the other bag, wondering what it could be.

"It's for you," Tanner said from behind her. "You don't need to open it yet."

"What is it?"

Becky came running. "I know what it is, but it's a surprise. Open it."

Eva glanced at Tanner, not sure what to do. They'd made their statements to each other very clear.

"You can open it," he said. "We want you to."

Thinking he was doing this for Becky's sake, Eva sank down on the bench by the table. "I don't need any gifts, Tanner."

"You do, too," Becky said. "Daed said you've been a blessing to us, so this is something for you. Something very special."

Her heart bumped and tossed inside her chest, causing Eva to gulp a breath. She wouldn't have a panic attack over a gift. So she did what she'd done all day. She took a deep breath and calmed herself down. She'd matured a lot since arriving here. She could do this with grace and a proper decorum.

Not a panic attack and a lovesick heart.

Becky took Tanner's hand while they stood watching her. That scene almost did Eva in. How could she leave them?

She carefully untied the white twine that held the paper over the gift. Whatever was inside felt heavy, like wood.

As she tore the paper away, her eyes widened in disbelief. She could smell the sweet scent of cedar, but that wasn't what took her breath away.

The beautifully carved flower sitting in the center of the oval slat of wood caused her to gasp. "A hibiscus?"

"For you," Becky said, clapping her hands.

"I heard they are your favorite," Tanner said.

"You made this, for me?" Eva didn't want to cry but she just might. The man couldn't say anything much with words, so he did what came naturally. He made her a special carving. Just for her. Could it be his way of telling her he cared?

"Do you like it?" Becky asked, her hands up against her face.

"I love it." Eva touched her fingers to the pink petals. They looked so delicate, but the wood was sturdy, and it had been shellacked to shining perfection. "My very own hibiscus flower."

Eva gently placed the carving on the table then held her arms open for Becky. The girl rushed to her, and they hugged.

"Denke," Eva whispered. "I will cherish this forever."

Becky bobbed her head, then glanced at Tanner. "You need to hug Daed. He made it. I just helped him keep the secret."

"Well, your father and you sure are *gut* at that," Eva said, still holding Becky.

But the girl meant business. She pulled back and grabbed her *daed*'s hand. "Hugs?"

Tanner looked sheepish as he lifted Eva off the bench and pulled her close. Eva fell against him, the scent of wood and the ocean all around him. She'd dream of that *wunderbar* smell long after she'd returned home.

Tanner held her tight while her heartbeat trembled against his chest. Then he pulled back, that stoic expression replacing the longing that hovered over and around him.

"We should go," he said. "It's getting late."

Becky motioned. "Look at the sunset. Martha says that's *Gott*'s way of telling us to go to sleep. He's turning the lights out."

"And He does it with an amazing hand," Eva said, her voice shaky after the gift and that hug. She wanted to turn back to Tanner and tell him she'd stay forever, but she didn't do that.

Tanner stood with her and Becky as they watched

the gold-and-blue hues merge together over the azure water. It did look like a painting.

"I'll never forget this place," Eva said.

"Because you'll *kumm* back," Becky reminded her. "I just know you will."

"I will," Eva said. But in her heart, she felt as if this might be the last time she ever stood here with this man and child. All the more reason to cherish her beautiful hibiscus even more.

Chapter Twenty-Two

The next few weeks became a routine for Eva. One that
ebbed and flowed like the nearby waters. Her heart shat-
tered like those great sea waves each time she thought
about leaving Pinecraft.

Leaving Tanner and Becky.

*Father Gott, I came here to feel better and see this
beautiful place my* aenti *always talks about, but I never
dreamed I'd fall in love with the first man who ever
paid much attention to me, and his little daughter, too.
Help me to be brave. Help me to let go and go home.
And please send them someone who can love them and
care for them.*

She prayed this prayer day and night while she and
Teresa helped Ramona as her business stayed steady
during the beginning of the high season. Tourists
crowded the streets and the beaches, and many of them
came into the Dawson Department Store.

Eva continued to work there for a few hours when
she could, and she walked to school to get Becky, so
they could talk about their day, just the two of them.
Then they'd have a break on their picnic table, Tanner

joining them at times even if he barely spoke and often looked off into the distance.

But for the most part, he stayed busy, too. "Business always picks up in the spring," he'd told Eva one day when he needed her to stay with Becky later than usual. "I don't know when I'll be done and home. I have to hang a huge wooden fish on a wall."

"I'll be here," Eva had said, wishing that to be true. Wishing they could be carefree and laughing the way they'd been on the beach when he'd given her the beautiful carving.

It had a place of honor on the small dresser in her bedroom at Ramona's house. Eva touched it each time she walked by it, remembering the look in Tanner's eyes when she opened it. The pretty pink hibiscus jutted out from the shiny wood like a real flower perched on a branch. It looked so real with its yellow face and hot pink blossoms. So real.

Was anything about this real?

Now as she sat on the back porch watching Becky chasing butterflies, Eva let herself think more about Tanner.

He cared. She could see that, and because she could see that, she'd tried to wait him out. He had to work through his feelings. She'd showed up here and he'd been the first person she'd met. But a man settled in his ways, and stubborn at that, might not ever make the first move.

Should she?

Neh. She'd rather just leave than to be rejected by Tanner. She'd get over this and she'd have her memories. But when she thought about going home to the routines her mother mandated, Eva cringed. She'd lived a different life here—her life.

But was this the life *Gott* planned for her?

Unsure and confused, she could at least enjoy her last few days with Becky. She often sat in the swing with Becky, waiting for Tanner to come home. That gave her time to wonder what was holding them back, what was between them that couldn't let them talk about their feelings for each other.

Well, there was her mother, who had become impatient and demanding again. "You should have been home a month ago. Are you planning to never return?"

"I'll be there soon." She explained about Becky's school program. "I have to be there when she sings."

"You need to be here. Not there spending time with a widowed man who is older than you."

Eva didn't try to point out that a lot of Amish women married older men, and for the most part, their families approved.

Finally, out of frustration, Eva asked Helen, "And what about you? How is Moses?"

For once, her *mamm* had been speechless. "What do you mean? He's fine."

"I mean, you talk about him more than you ever have. Have you two finally made your peace?"

"Perhaps. We are civil."

"I see. Civil is a start, ain't so?"

"I miss my child. Moses is my neighbor. I can be civil to him as any neighbor ought to, but you should obey me and get yourself home."

"I miss you, too, Mamm," Eva had told her this morning. "I'll be there soon, and we will make tea and have a *gut* talk."

"I'd like that," Helen had said. "And Eva, Ramona goes on and on about what a help you are to her. She's proud of you and well… I am, too. Now don't dawdle. You have a busy day."

Her *mamm*, ever the surprising one. Kind one moment and angry the next. Eva decided she was caught between two worlds, the one she wanted and the one her *mamm* wanted for her. How could she ever choose?

Tanner was stuck in the past, needing a wife but longing for the one he'd lost. He might not ever admit his true feelings. Someone had to decide something here.

Well, she'd decided and that meant she'd go home the day after Becky's program. Teresa had spent a lot of time with Eva and Becky. Eva knew Teresa would be a big help to the child.

But Becky didn't seem so sure. She liked Teresa, but the child had it in her head that Eva should be her *mamm*.

Now Becky giggled as she tried to catch a swallowtail. They left their larvae on the citrus trees which would then become heavy with what was called orange-dog caterpillars, created from a tiny orange egg. It was amazing that the strange-looking chrysalis turned into a beautiful butterfly. No wonder Becky loved them.

"I almost caught it," she squealed. "But I don't want to break its wings."

Eva waved and smiled. She felt like that butterfly. She'd been enclosed in the chrysalis of her mother's overbearing love and demands, cocooned and protected, but arriving here had helped her shed that delicate skin and lift her wings to the sky. She'd felt free for the first time in her life.

Am I wrong, Gott? *Am I wrong to want to spread my wings and find the life I pray for? Or will my frag-*

*ile wings be broken? Help me—show me the way. Your
will, my prayers.*

Eva said her silent prayer and hoped the Lord would
guide her along the right path.

When she opened her eyes, Tanner was standing on
the porch by the back door, staring at her with those
big eyes that held the depth of the ocean. Those eyes
held as many secrets as the ocean, too. Eva had tried to
read those secrets, and she'd failed. Maybe that was her
answer then. She would accept that and go back home
to Campton Creek.

Tanner couldn't stop thinking about how much he
wanted to rush to Eva and beg her to stay. But he didn't
have the right to do that. He'd tried love once and he'd
failed miserably. He couldn't make Deborah love him,
and he hadn't protected her enough to keep her alive.
Never mind that the doctors said she'd had a complicated pregnancy and had gone through a hard birthing.

Becky had survived. Her *mamm* hadn't. No one's
fault.

Gott's will, they all said.

Or some sort of tribulation for the lies they'd both
held in their hearts. Maybe if he confessed everything
to Eva, he'd finally be free of the pain and the guilt,
the horrible never-ending grief. Maybe. But what if he
couldn't let it all go?

He would not hurt this woman, this sweet, tender,
gentle, loving young woman who desired so much more
than he could give.

He'd rather let her go, than see her turn away as
Deborah had done.

So he stood silent and watchful, taking in the warm
spring air and the scent of flowers blooming. He no-

ticed Becky laughing and singing to the butterflies; he noticed Eva in her mint-green dress, her hair tidy under the stark white *kapp*.

Eva came to stand by him. "She sang *wunderbar gut* at practice today, Tanner. I can't wait for you to hear her."

Tanner nodded. "I hope I can make it. I have this big order that has to be delivered that day."

"You must be there," Eva said. "She'll be heartbroken if you don't show up."

Tanner's worry for Becky got the best of him. "I've always tried to show up when my daughter is concerned. You don't have to point that out to me."

"I'm sorry." Eva's pretty face held a light blush. "I should go."

Regretting his outburst, Tanner tugged at her arm. "I know you mean well."

"But you don't want anyone else here with you and Becky, because you're so afraid you can't make the rules or protect her if someone else steps in—even me."

"Eva?"

"I get it, Tanner. You and I haven't talked since we decided to part ways, but I get it now. You never had any intentions other than needing someone to watch Becky. Well, I've watched her, and I've seen what she can become—not what you're trying to make her. I had to leave home to see that in myself and now I sure see it in your child."

"You don't understand," he said, trying to form the words to tell her so many things.

She pulled away but he tugged her close and without thinking, he kissed her, and was completely caught off guard when Eva responded. They stood there, hidden from Becky by a big lush palm tree in a huge pot. He held her close, and she wrapped arms around his neck, tugging his head down.

Right then and there, Tanner thought he could break a lot of rules—for this woman.

This was the perfect scene of serenity and calm, a facade of the life he believed he'd have. And then, off in the distance, lightning hit the sky over the trees.

Becky screamed came running toward the porch as the boom of thunder followed. "Daed!"

Tanner let go of Eva and hurried down the steps and grabbed Becky close. "It's okay. Just a storm coming in from the gulf."

"I'm glad you're home," Becky said as they came up onto the porch. "Eva's here, too. Don't let her leave."

Tanner glanced at Eva and saw the longing and the surprise in her eyes and that soft blush on her cheeks. Followed by regret. "I didn't notice that dark cloud behind the house."

"It came on quickly." Tanner set Becky on her feet, thinking that kiss had come on quickly, too. "Rain is coming in from the west, but it snuck up on us."

Eva glanced at the darkening sky. "I should get home then, before it turns worse. Your supper is on the stove and Becky has done her homework and she has practiced her singing."

There was a silent moment between them, like the time between the lightning followed by the thunder, a moment where Tanner hoped Eva would see the love in his heart.

"I want inside," Becky said, breaking the tension as the sky continued to roar.

Tanner knew these pop-up showers didn't last long, but he also knew his kiss had confused Eva even more than his outburst. "Maybe you should wait."

"I can't wait, Tanner. I'll run ahead of the storm."

Her words had more meaning than she'd said.

"Eva?"

She took off into the house before he could ask her to stay. By the time he and Becky made it to the kitchen, Eva was waving to them from the open front door. "See you tomorrow."

Tanner hadn't missed the determination in her words.

Eva Miller was tired of waiting.

Eva checked the sky. An ominous dark cloud hovered like a giant mushroom toward the southwest. She should make it home before the storm got here if she ran quickly. She'd only made it a few yards up the sidewalk when the rain hit. Big cold drops plummeted at her as she tried to step through water in her flimsy flip-flops. Drenched within seconds, Eva took off her shoes and dropped them in her soaked tote bag. She hurried barefoot toward the other side of town, thinking she hadn't taken this rain seriously. She should have waited it out at Tanner's house.

But her heart couldn't take that. Not after the way he'd kissed her, and not after she'd responded in a way that told him how much she cared. A kiss was one thing, but honesty was quite another. He still held back that spot in his heart where he'd buried his secrets. He'd never allow anyone else to love Becky. Or him.

Now she was soaked through and cold, and discovering that even in a mild climate a rainstorm could make a body shiver. She was about to turn the corner toward Ramona's home when a man on a fancy bike came barreling toward her. Eva screamed but the man didn't see her or hear her until it was too late. They collided, the front of the bike hitting Eva and sending her into the nearby bird-of-paradise bushes before the man swerved and took a tumble onto the sidewalk.

Eva hit hard against a hidden cement curb and stumbled forward. She fell to the wet earth, blinked once and then everything went dark.

Chapter Twenty-Three

Tanner heard the knock at the door, wondering who'd be out on a rainy night like this.

He opened it to find Teresa and Jasper standing there underneath umbrellas, their expressions haggard.

"What's wrong?" he asked, his heart going heavy with dread.

"There was an accident," Teresa said. "Eva and a man on a racer bike. Just around the corner from Ramona's house. Eva was hurt."

Tanner grabbed for something, anything. He held to the open door. "And?"

"I'm here to stay with Becky," Teresa said. "Jasper will get you to the hospital. Ramona is already there."

Tanner heard a distant drumming and realized it was his pulse. "Hospital? Just tell me how bad it is. Is Eva all right?"

"She's unconscious," Jasper said. "That's all we know right now. I've called a cab."

Tanner nodded, grabbed his hat and glanced at Teresa. "Becky is asleep. If she wakes—"

"I'll explain you got called away. Work."

Tanner didn't argue with that. He'd need to be the one to tell Becky if.

He wouldn't think about anything like that now. His brain wouldn't allow that. But he knew in his heart, Eva had run out of his home to get away from him. Him and his refusal to tell her he loved her. And to confess all his secrets and fears to her, too.

Tanner couldn't believe this. Why had he let her go out the door? Why? Because he was too broken, too terrified to love anyone again. He'd poured his heart and soul into loving his child to the point of smothering her the way Eva's *mamm* had smothered her. It was one thing to love a child but another to hold that child back. If Eva hadn't been involved, Becky wouldn't even be singing in the scholar program next week.

Next week. What would happen now?

He glanced up from his seat in the waiting room and wished he could turn the clock back, but it was too late for that. Too late for him to tell Eva everything. He'd go to the bishop and wipe this stain off his consciousness, do what needed to be done to find forgiveness and peace.

Now he prayed Eva would be all right and he'd have that same opportunity with her, too.

Ramona came walking back from the cafeteria, carrying two cups of coffee. She handed one to Tanner and then sat down beside him with her own. "I should have asked if you were hungry," she said.

"I'm not." He took a sip of the coffee and set the cup down on the table between them. "I wish I'd kept her at my house."

Ramona held her coffee cup with both hands. "If we're gonna play that game, I should have never forced her to come here in the first place."

"*Neh*, I'm glad she came to Pinecraft," he began. Then he shut up and leaned back against the cold wall.

Ramona wouldn't let that go. "Because?"

He slanted his gaze toward her, but he couldn't find the words. "I..."

"Let me do the talking," his friend said. "Because you think that keeping the truth about Becky's birth a secret is the best thing for everyone. You can't let anyone else into your life because then you'd have to be honest, and that might shed a bad light on Becky, right?"

He barely nodded. "*Ja*," came the raw whisper.

Ramona finally set her own cup down. "Becky is a sweet little girl with a hardworking *daed*. I know of no one here who has ever thought any less of her, regardless of the rumors that are always floating around. We love her, Tanner. We love our own, take care of our own. Don't you think it's time you let us do that and let *Gott* get on with his plan for you and your daughter?"

Ramona had never been one to mince words.

He thought about that for a while and then he said, "I love Eva. I do. But now I've messed things up with her in the same way I messed things up with Deborah."

"Deborah was a troubled woman," Ramona replied. "Eva seems levelheaded and capable. I know she has a lot of love to give."

Tanner lifted off the wall and rubbed his eyes. "Deborah did have problems. She didn't love me, Ramona. She only married me for Becky's sake."

"I know that much at least. Didn't take a lot to figure that out."

And yet, she'd never once let on. "You're a kind woman."

"So is Eva. What's holding you back?"

He couldn't tell her now. *Neh*, first he had to tell

Eva. Then he'd go to the bishop and confess all. If Eva was okay and still wanted him after that, he'd gladly ask her to be his wife.

"I need to clear my conscience. With Eva and with the brethren."

"Okay then, that's settled. Let's pray for Eva. I had to call Helen and she says she's coming down here on the first bus she can get to, and that she's taking her daughter home with her."

Tanner shook his head. "If she does, I promise you this. I will go to Campton Creek, and I will find Eva and I will bring her home, where she belongs."

"That's the Tanner I know," Ramona said with a soft smile. "Now drink your coffee. It's gonna be a long night."

Eva woke with a start, the sunshine beaming through the window blinds making her blink. She moaned and glanced around. Her head hurt and she ached all over. Staring down, she realized she wasn't at home, not even at Ramona's house. This looked like a hospital room.

"What's going on?" she asked, wondering if anyone could hear her.

"You're awake. Ramona, she's awake."

"Mamm?"

Helen stood and leaned over her. "I'm here, Eva. I'm here and you're going to be okay. Once you're up and about, I'm taking you home where you'll be safe."

No hello, so glad you're awake and I'm here to show you my love and to comfort you. *Neh*, not from Helen Miller.

Eva was too confused and disoriented to argue.

Ramona came to the other side of the bed. "You were

in an accident two days ago. The storm got bad, and you were on your way back to my place."

Eva nodded. "The rain. I couldn't see. A man on a bike."

"She's remembering," Ramona said to Helen. "That's a *gut* sign."

"*Ja*, he near killed you," Mamm said. "Whoever heard of such."

Ramona took Eva's hand. "You've got a sprained ankle and you hit your head on the concrete, but the doctor thinks you'll be okay. No concussion. Those huge bird-of-paradise bushes cushioned your fall."

Eva felt her bandaged left temple. "That's sore."

"You could have died," Mamm said, clucking her tongue. "Running in the rain like that. You'll catch a cold, mark my words."

Eva blinked again, her memories swirling like the sunshine slipping through the blind slats. She might be bruised and sore, but she definitely didn't have a cough or a cold. Instead, a warm blush of a memory poured through her tattered mind. He'd kissed her, but it had come at a cost and that kiss had come too late.

"Tanner? Becky?"

Helen huffed and straightened Eva's blanket. "I told that man to leave. He has no business here, hovering around. Sounds like it was his fault since you'd been at his home, watching his child. That's not proper, Eva. And now look what's happened."

Ramona glanced at her sister. "Helen, let the girl get her bearings. Why don't you go check on Moses? He's awfully tired."

"Moses? You brought Moses to Florida with you?" Eva asked, her mind clearing as she went. "I'm going to be okay, Mamm."

"I had to be sure, didn't I?" Helen asked, tears in her eyes. "And Moses insisted on coming with me. That's a mighty long bus ride when you're worried your daughter might be—"

"—I'm okay, Mamm," Eva interjected. "I'm sorry you came all this way."

Her mother stared down at her. "Just get well so we can go home. You can't stay here. It isn't safe and I don't care what your doctor back home thinks."

Eva grew weary just thinking about what "back home" would be like now. But she didn't have the energy to dispute her *mamm*.

Ramona took over. "Helen, we need to let the nurses know Eva is awake. Go find someone."

Helen marched to the door and took off.

Ramona leaned in and whispered to Eva. "You drifted in and out yesterday. Tanner went home and then came back right after your *mamm* and Moses arrived. Fancy that."

"And she sent him away?"

"She did," Ramona said. "Told him you didn't want him here."

Eva's fingers clutched the soft blanket, her mind spinning in a whirl of despair. Did she want him here? If not, that was her decision, not Mamm's. "Did he believe her?"

"I don't know. Right now, he can't believe in himself, so he didn't fight her too much. He feels responsible and I fear he's having some flashbacks, being back in this hospital."

"Deborah died here?"

"*Ja*, and Becky was born here."

Tanner would surely be in his own pit of despair. But what could she do, lying here and barely able to move? Mamm had sent him away. Eva had to get a knock on the head to see that she loved the man, and that she should stand firm in that love. But would that even matter?

"He's never going to admit that he loves me," Eva said, tears in her eyes. "He didn't even protest my mother's words. I think I do need to go home, after all."

Ramona patted her arm. "That man might not be able to say the words, but honey, he is in love with you. Right now, he's just scared to death of messing things up again."

Eva nodded, fatigue taking over. "I'll explain things to him if I ever see him again." Then she drifted back to sleep, oblivious to her *mamm*'s sharp orders to the nurses.

Over the next few days, Tanner worked with the desperation of a man running from the truth. He carved and painted and arranged wood and driftwood and seashells until he'd made enough items to fill a whole shelf out front. He had frames covered with seashells; he had mirrors layered with starfish and shells. He'd cleaned and carved biscuit bowls and bread trays, and candleholders. Busywork, that's all it was.

And still he'd heard nothing from Eva.

He should have given the message to Ramona that day at the hospital when he'd returned, but she'd gone home to take care of some things and instead, he'd heard the wrath of Eva's *mamm*. Helen would not tell Eva what he'd said. And he knew that. Maybe he'd sabotaged himself on purpose.

"I care about her..." he'd stuttered, his emotions too raw to make a complete sentence. "It's my fault. I should let her go...but I can't. I care. Please...tell her that."

Helen had given him a cold stare. "I'll think about telling her, but my child is not going to want to stay here—not after this. She'll be going home with me, mark my words."

Tanner wanted to go back to the hospital, but he had work to do. Always work to do. And Becky was asking too many questions. Teresa had been a great help there, as well as Martha and his other family members.

But Becky wanted Eva. And so did he.

He planned to go talk to the bishop today, and he planned to see Eva soon, no matter what her *mamm* said. Then he'd tell Eva the truth—all of the truth. But he'd also tell her he loved her with all his heart and soul, and he trusted her to help raise his child. And he'd pray she loved him back.

Chapter Twenty-Four

The next day, the doctor told Eva she could go home as long as she took it easy. Her *mamm* stood with Ramona in her room, waiting for the discharge papers.

"I have everything under control," Mamm said now. "Ramona and I gathered your things this morning. Moses had bought the bus tickets. We can leave as soon as we get those papers. We're breaking the trip up and stopping at hotels for the night so you can rest."

Eva waited for the part where Mamm would remind her of how much this trip had cost, with doctor visits and now, a hospital stay. But Mamm hadn't fussed at her too much. Probably that would happen once they were away from Pinecraft.

"Helen, why don't you all stay until the weekend," Ramona suggested. "Eva is still bruised and sore. She shouldn't get on a bus yet."

Helen huffed a breath. "I want to get her away from the temptation this place holds. I told you, we'll stop so Eva can rest, but we need to leave. And soon."

Ramona stood by her sister, distress on her usually jovial face. Glancing at Eva, she said, "Teresa is going to try and make it by to see you before you go. She is handing Becky off to Martha."

"The scholar program," Eva said, tears forming in her eyes. "That's today?"

"Ja," Ramona said. "Becky is taking it hard that you won't be there."

"What's this?" Mamm asked, her tone stern and ready to argue.

Eva looked at her hands. "Becky's school is holding a singing. She's performing a short solo during the program. Some of it is in High German, but we know the songs well. Her solo is in *Englisch.* I promised her I'd be there."

"You can't do that," Mamm said. "Our bus leaves at three."

"The program starts at two-thirty," Ramona said. "You might catch part of it."

"Neh, she is to be at the bus station, not rushing around to see a school program." She held her head high. "That way, we can stop for the night in Atlanta. Moses has found accommodations for us, two rooms. Then we go on tomorrow with a possible stop in Nashville. Moses wants to see a few things in the city. I can stay with Eva in the hotel room unless she just wants to sleep. Then I might walk around with Moses."

"When did you get so adventurous?" Ramona asked while Eva stared up at her mother in shock.

Mamm shrugged. "I had to find something to fill my time."

Eva glanced from her mother to Ramona. "I'd like to speak to Mamm alone, Aenti."

Ramona gave her an encouraging nod. "Of course, dear."

Mamm stared after her sister. "What now?"

Eva sat up against her pillow, her dress clean and her apron tied. Ramona had combed her hair and braided it neatly so she could put on her *kapp*. She still had a bandage on her temple and a compression wrap on her sore ankle, but she could walk on her own. The man on the bicycle had visited her this morning.

"I'm so glad you're okay," he told her after offering to pay her hospital bills, which she'd refused. "I shouldn't have been going so fast in that rain." He'd brought flowers. Pink lilies and roses. Which only reminded her of the hibiscus carving Tanner had made her. "Did you pack my hibiscus?" she asked Helen.

Mamm looked confused. "I don't know. Ramona packed most of your things while Moses and I got the bus tickets and made our arrangements."

"I can't leave without that," Eva said, trying to stand. "Tanner made it for me. He's a *gut* man, Mamm. I love him and Becky. He made me a special gift—a pretty flower carved out of wood. I have to find it."

"Calm down, child," Mamm said, worry in her eyes. "I'm sure Ramona can mail it if it's not packed."

"Mamm, I don't want to go home," Eva said. "They need me, and I've done fine here except for a little cold and getting hit by a bike in the rainstorm. I know you love me, but I need my own life. I will always love you and I'm willing to help you with anything, but I really like it here and… I don't know. I just don't want to go with things so unsettled."

"This is not right," Mamm said. "You might think you're in love, but where is this Tanner person? He has not been around."

"Because you sent him away," Eva said, standing up, her hands gripping the bed railing. "I'm not leaving Pinecraft until I see Tanner and Becky. And I know where they'll both be this afternoon."

Tanner was late. But he had a good reason. After he'd delivered and hung the huge fish he'd pieced together out of driftwood and some sea glass his client had collected from Lake Erie over the years, he'd hurried to see the bishop.

Bishop Lapp was a kind man who seemed to stay calm in any kind of chaos. Tanner remembered how the bishop and his wife had been so thoughtful to him after Deborah's death. Ruth Lapp had taken Becky into her arms and cooed to her while they'd talked about nothing at all.

Today, he'd sat across from Bishop Lapp and explained his predicament. Once he was finished, the bishop had nodded, his hands clasped together.

"You will need to come before the brethren and tell this story, Tanner. And you know you'll be forgiven. You made a hard choice, but the right choice for Becky's sake. You are her father in every way." Then he'd added, "You must pray on these things, and I will pray, too. You're a valuable member of this community and you provide jobs for people. I think you can rest assured now. And if things turn out *gut* with you and our Eva, then God's will can prevail."

Now Tanner hurried along the streets, his cart sputtering as he tried to get to Becky's program before she sang. He knew if he missed this, Eva would not forgive him. But then, Eva probably wouldn't be there, would she?

He'd heard from Teresa that she might leave this afternoon.

He couldn't go chasing after her at the bus stop when

he had to be at Becky's event. Or could he? Checking his watch, he knew the answer to that.

He'd chosen Becky every time, he thought. Eva had encouraged this—that he'd be at the scholar singing. Why couldn't he have chosen Eva, too?

He could have a wife and take care of Becky. In fact, he needed a wife to help him take care of his daughter, but he'd always been afraid a new wife would frown on Becky's birth if she knew he wasn't Becky's real father.

He was a block from the school, but he was also a block from the bus stop. Tanner groaned and took a left turn. He could check the bus stop and still make it to the school just in time if he hurried.

When he pulled up to the bus station, his heart dropped. There stood Eva and her mother with the older man Moses. They must be about to board the bus.

Tanner stared at them, wishing he could approach Eva without her mother there. Torn, he didn't know what to do. He had to get to the school.

He took one last gaze at Eva, thinking he'd never see her again. But she looked up and around, as if she knew he might be there. When she saw him, she waved and hurried to him, her ankle wrapped and obviously still painful.

Her *mamm* and Moses turned around. Helen looked at him and then she glanced at Eva. And she smiled.

Eva couldn't believe her eyes. Tanner had come to see her off. Only she wasn't leaving. She hurried as fast as possible with her sore ankle, careful not to trip or make it worse. Tanner saw her coming and pulled the cart up close, then jumped off. "Eva?"

"Tanner?"

He rushed to her and held her in his arms. "Don't

leave, Eva. We have just enough time to see Becky sing. You promised you'd be there. If you have to leave, you can take another bus."

Before she could speak, he added, "And I need to tell you everything. Everything, okay. First, I went to the bishop and told him my story, and I'll tell my confession when church meets again. I... I love you so much...and I don't want you to go. But there is more."

Eva put her finger to his lips, touched by how he'd struggled to get all of that out. "Tanner, I'm not leaving. I was telling Mamm and Moses goodbye. They're going home, but they're taking the long way home and then they are to be married this fall. Possibly here in Pinecraft."

Tanner seemed to have missed the fact that Eva's mother had a whole new life and was leaving. He grabbed her up into his arms. "You're staying."

"I was staying for Becky's program, *ja*. But after what you just declared, I'd say I'm staying for a long, long time." She held his head in her hands. "Because I was also staying for you, Tanner. I love you, too. So much."

He looked relieved and confused, his brows burrowing together. "But I haven't told you all the truth."

"We'll have a lifetime for that. Right now, we are needed elsewhere."

Tanner nodded. Eva turned and waved to her *mamm*. Helen smiled and nodded, then wiped at her eyes. Moses waved and they got on the bus, merging with the other passengers.

Eva stared after the bus, her heart pounding. "They're really leaving." She wasn't sure Mamm could actually do it.

"How did you pull that off?" Tanner asked as he pushed the cart to its limit. "I told the truth," she said, laughing, her heart so light she thought she might fly. "I told Mamm I loved you and I was going to stay here and fight for you. She balked until…until she heard me crying and found Moses trying to comfort me. Then she came into the room and confessed that she and Moses want to marry, but she was concerned about me. I told her I'd be fine, and we worked it out. They will come and visit often, and they did talk about getting married here. She realized we love each other in the same way she finally admitted she loved Moses. And Moses is beyond in love with her. Life sure is funny, ain't so."

"For certain sure," Tanner said. "But Eva, after the program I'll tell you the rest of my story."

"I know the rest of your story," she replied, so happy. "But I will listen anyway."

Becky sang such a sweet rendition of "Jesus Loves Me," everyone in the room had tears flowing down their faces. When the other children joined in, more tears came.

Tanner held Eva's hand, his misty gaze moving from her back to Becky. Ramona and all of Tanner's family had come, too. Becky beamed and went on to sing with the rest of the children as if nothing special had happened.

When it was over, she ran up to Eva and Tanner. "You're here. You both came."

Tanner took his daughter into his arms. "*Ja*, and you were *wunderbar gut*. All of you."

Becky showed humility. "My friends sang so pretty, too. And Daed, you had Eva with you, ain't so?"

"I did," Tanner said, smiling. "And Eva is going to stay with us for a long, long time."

Becky squealed, causing others to glance at them and smile. "Eva, you stretched it?"

They all laughed. "I did stretch it—for a lifetime."

They headed to the park to celebrate the end of school with Teresa's family. It seemed the whole community had shown up with food and drinks. Isaac kept everyone moving and organized, and soon they were all eating ice cream and playing shuffleboard.

Becky was off playing with her friends, Teresa and Jasper watching out for her while Tanner took Eva off toward the creek.

He found a bench and they sat down.

"I love you," he said. "I don't know why that was so hard to admit."

"I love you, too, and I don't mind admitting that."

He turned to her then and told her all about Deborah's forbidden affair with an *Englisch*. "He was a rookie officer, Eva. A police officer. He knew he'd be in trouble for messing with an Amish girl, and then she got pregnant. They'd planned to leave together, but he got shot while serving a warrant."

"He died?" Eva's heart seemed to shatter all over again. "Tanner, what a horrible thing to happen." Suddenly, Eva understood everything. "So she came to you?"

He nodded. "She knew I loved her. And she knew I'd marry her, no matter."

"I see it all now. You had to protect Becky. Are you afraid her other grandparents will find her?"

"*Neh*. The officer wasn't close to his family and after I'd tracked them down, just in case they ever came calling, I found out the grandfather had died, and the grandmama had dementia and was in a nursing home. So I never said anything to anyone. I was more afraid for Becky. That she'd be ridiculed or teased or worse, shunned, if anyone ever found out my secret. But I am her father. I will always be her father."

Eva leaned close and he wrapped his arm around her shoulder and held her there. Off in the distance the sunset hovered over the palm trees and winked behind the tall pines. "Becky will be just fine, Tanner. Because I will love her and protect her same as you."

He tugged Eva's chin up with his thumb. "So you'll marry me?"

"I will."

"And Becky might have some siblings one day?"

"I sure hope so."

"Can you forgive me?"

"Nothing to forgive other than your grumpy nature."

Tanner leaned over and kissed her. Leaving her breathless, he whispered, "Hmm. Seems my grumpy nature has disappeared."

They laughed and held each other while the sun set out over the sea, taking their secrets with it, but leaving a beautiful afterglow for them to enjoy while they held each other tight.

* * * * *

Dear Reader,

I moved to Florida a decade ago and I love it here. I grew up in Southwest Georgia, near the Georgia–Florida line, so I visited the coast of Florida growing up. This beautiful state has always held a part of my heart. But I'd never traveled much of the state beyond the panhandle. The peninsula is also beautiful, and Sarasota is one of those beautiful spots. Pinecraft is a small community of Amish in this area. It started as a fishing camp and getaway during the winter and has now grown into a quaint Amish village. What better place to write about the Amish?

Especially a story about a young woman who'd never left Campton Creek, Pennsylvania. Eva wanted to see the world, so when her doctor and her aunt encouraged her, she took off to Pinecraft and found her heart. Tanner loved this place, too. But he couldn't relax and enjoy the beauty around him. He worried too much and tried to protect his child. I'm glad these two found each other and I know Eva will be a great source of love for Tanner and Becky.

Life is like that sometimes. When I first moved to Florida, as much as I loved it, I missed the life I'd left behind in Louisiana. But one day I looked out the window and thought, *Lenora, you live about six miles from the Gulf of Mexico. Start enjoying it.* So I did. I have always believed in blooming where you're planted. If you're in a spot where you're unsure about things, remember to look up and see the beauty around you. It's there. Eva and Tanner found it. I hope you will, too.

Until next time, may the angels watch over you. Always.
Lenora Worth.

COMING NEXT MONTH FROM
Love Inspired

THEIR AMISH SECRET
Amish Country Matches • by Patricia Johns

Putting the past behind her is all single Amish mother Claire Glick wants. But when old love Joel Beiler shows up on her doorstep in the middle of a harrowing storm, it could jeopardize everything she's worked for—including her best-kept secret...

THE QUILTER'S SCANDALOUS PAST
by Patrice Lewis

Esther Yoder's family must sell their mercantile store, and when an out-of-town buyer expresses interest, Esther is thrilled. Then she learns the buyer is Joseph Kemp—the man responsible for ruining her reputation. Can she set aside her feelings for the sake of the deal?

THE RANCHER'S SANCTUARY
K-9 Companions • by Linda Goodnight

With zero ranching experience, greenhorn Nathan Garrison has six months to reopen an abandoned guest ranch—or lose it forever. So he hires scarred cowgirl Monroe Matheson to show him the ropes. As they work together, will secrets from the past ruin their chance at love?

THE BABY INHERITANCE
Lazy M Ranch • by Tina Radcliffe

Life changes forever when rancher Drew Morgan inherits his best friend's baby. But when he learns professor Sadie Ross is also part of the deal, things get complicated. Neither one of them is ready for domestic bliss, but sweet baby Mae might change their minds...

MOTHER FOR A MONTH
by Zoey Marie Jackson

Career-weary Sienna King yearns to become a mother, and opportunity knocks when know-it-all reporter Joel Armstrong comes to her with an unusual proposal. Putting aside their differences, they must work together to care for his infant nephew, but what happens when their pretend family starts to feel real?

THE NANNY NEXT DOOR
Second Chance Blessings • by Jenna Mindel

Grieving widower Jackson Taylor moves to small-town Michigan for the sake of his girls. When he hires his attractive next-door neighbor, Maddie Williams, to be their nanny, it could be more than he bargained for as the line between personal and professional starts to blur...

LOOK FOR THESE AND OTHER LOVE INSPIRED BOOKS WHEREVER BOOKS ARE SOLD, INCLUDING MOST BOOKSTORES, SUPERMARKETS, DISCOUNT STORES AND DRUGSTORES.

LICNM0323

HARLEQUIN
PLUS

Try the best multimedia
subscription service for romance
readers like you!

Read, Watch and Play.

Experience the easiest way to get
the romance content you crave.

Start your **FREE TRIAL** at
<u>www.harlequinplus.com/freetrial</u>.